The Shadow Doctor

ADRIAN PLASS

The Shadow Doctor

HODDER &
STOUGHTON

First published in Great Britain in 2017 by Hodder & Stoughton
An Hachette UK company

1

Copyright © Adrian Plass, 2017

The right of Adrian Plass to be identified as the Author of the Work has been
asserted by him in accordance with the Copyright, Designs and Patents Act 1988.

A CIP catalogue record for this title is available from the British Library

ISBN 978 1 444 74547 4
eBook 978 1 444 74548 1

Typeset in Sabon MT by Hewer Text UK Ltd, Edinburgh

Printed and bound in the UK by CPI Group (UK) Ltd, Croydon CR0 4YY

Hodder & Stoughton policy is to use papers that are natural, renew-
able and recyclable products and made from wood grown in sustain-
able forests. The logging and manufacturing processes are expected to
conform to the environmental regulations of the country of origin.

Hodder & Stoughton Ltd
Carmelite House
50 Victoria Embankment
London EC4Y 0DZ

www.hodderfaith.com

This book, probably the most difficult I have ever written, is dedicated to my friends, Liz, Ren and Chase. They have been supportive and inspirational.

Contents

Prologue

At two o'clock in the morning the man stepped out of his cottage, locking the door carefully behind him. A couple of strides away from the house, he stopped, pushed his gloved hands into his pockets and leaned the top part of his body back to stare up at the clear night sky. Clusters of tiny, exploding pinpoints filled the heavens. Endless stands of trees closely guarding the little dwelling remained watchful and dark, apparently unimpressed by starlight.

Shivering a little, the man set off briskly down the little sloping garden, across the patchy lawn, past the abandoned chicken run and the vegetable patch towards a gap in the trees where a narrow path gave access to the hidden heart of the forest. No hesitation. He knew every inch of the way. No fear of being lost.

That was not his fear.

Fifteen minutes later he stopped at a place where the path had no choice but to take a wide loop around a massive, toad-shaped chunk of limestone. Patting the face of the rock once with the palm of his hand, he turned away from the outside edge of the loop, ducking and weaving his way expertly through a confusion of more or less horizontal branches before emerging onto something that was more of an animal trail than a path. After a little careful negotiation he entered a clearing that was roughly circular in shape.

Standing in the centre of the small open space, the man wrapped his arms around his chest and lifted his eyes to stare at the natural planetarium above his head.

A minute passed. Something stirred and built in him. His whole body began to tremble. The shout of agony, when it came, crashed into the soullessly resistant trunks of the surrounding trees, ricocheting back towards the solitary figure.

'I'm frightened! It's too much – I don't think I can do it any more!'

There was no response to his desperate cry. Many sounds, but none that were directed at him. The man knew the voices of the forest well. The whispering, groaning language of the trees. Small creatures screaming in their own little worlds of agony or ecstasy. He knew the muffled thump of an owl's flight, the serrated edges of its wings allowing almost silent movement as it hunted small animals and birds on the forest floor. He recognised the loud, ventrilo-quial churr of the nightjar, to him the most mystically intriguing inhabitant of this crepuscular world. He was familiar with all of these voices. He was not afraid of them, and he was not afraid of the darkness.

That was not his fear.

So keenly attuned was he to the common noises of the night that the sound of a twig cracking on the edge of the clearing caused him to whip his head round in surprise. No conjecture. No need to guess the weight required to produce that particular noise. But it was an interference. It was a shock.

Only one person could have followed him into the forest.

I

Flame

After a long drive from the south and a failed appointment, Jack Merton found himself stranded one damp morning in the pocket-sized Yorkshire city of Ripon. At the end of an unevenly paved alley threading itself away from the tiny city centre he was abruptly confronted by the cathedral church of St Peter's. Crossing Minster Road, he ducked through the west door to escape the annoyingly persistent drizzle. Peace fell upon him as he stepped into the nave. Something of a benevolent shock. It was much more than the simple difference between being damp and being dry. The seam between one state and the other was impossible to detect. It was like magic. Magical.

'Wickedly magical,' he whispered to himself with delicious indulgence.

Jack's father had taught his young son to love English cathedrals. He always said that they revealed inadequacy through excess. Being in this one now was like standing inside a vast bell, filled with soft, friendly light and a host of shadows in every shade of grey, blending effortlessly from shy through to bold. No longer stranded, but simply present, Jack circled the building in a dream until he came across a mini Swiss alp of wrought-iron candle racks at the foot of a pillar opposite the south wall.

The very sight of candles disturbed him a little. Since becoming a believer at the age of sixteen, Jack had been trying not to allow such crudely visible symbols to add a dimension of reality to his prayers, however seductively hypnotic the sight and concept of a melting flame might seem. There was a general consensus in his circles that spirituality could only be truly authentic if it existed outside the world of 'things'. Recently, though, he had become vaguely aware of the contradictions in this notion. The church he had been attending for some years, for instance, had reverted to cherryade instead of wine when it came to Communion, but as far as Jack could see, the Holy Elements remained healthily solid and visible.

Now, in a spasm of independence, he dropped a pound into the slot below the racks, took one of the unused tealights from a nearby cardboard box and carefully lit it from a burning candle, releasing a sob of misery, quickly disguised as a little hack of a cough, as the wick caught.

In some inexplicable way the sob felt like a prayer. Outrageously, it was for himself. It was probably the most inchoate but profound supplication he had ever made. He watched the candle burn for a few seconds, enjoying it as if it were a personal achievement. Perhaps, he wondered, the almost undetectable but unarguably random movement of the tiny flame might prove to be a symbol of liberation, a possibility of something new, if he had the courage or the will to grasp it. But what on earth could that mean? At this moment, and in this place, he had no idea.

A fortnight later he would open and read his grandmother's letter. It was to change his life.

2

Alice

Jack's grandmother had died three months earlier, days before her ninetieth birthday. The Golden Hands carer, Barbara, who helped Alice to get up every weekday morning, had discovered the elderly lady, face pillowed on her hands, looking as rosy cheeked and peaceful as ever. Barbara wept a little. She had grown very fond of funny, feisty Alice. Difficult to accept that she would never wake again in this world.

Jack had always loved and appreciated his gran. She adored him, and much enjoyed telling people that her grandson was a good-looking young man with a charming smile and a schoolboy-shaped head who might easily be mistaken for the actor Matt Damon. She was a bright, unfading light in the darker tunnels of Jack's life, especially since the death of his father had left him alone in the world. She was always rapturously pleased to see him, always kind, always giving. She was good to talk with as well. Actually, more than good. There was a wit and an edge to Alice Merton's conversation that encouraged her inwardly uncertain grandson to explore tentatively some of the truths about himself that were definitely not for general release.

Jack hardly remembered William, his grandfather. There were photographs on the bureau in the sitting room

3

of the ground-floor Eastbourne flat that Gran had moved
to when stairs became too much for her. They showed a
tall, tweedy, smart man with incongruously untidy hair, a
confident smile and, in almost every image, a protective
arm placed firmly around his wife's shoulders. It had
amused Jack that, in every picture, Gran's wide-eyed,
beaming, oval portrait of a face seemed to be saying
breathlessly, 'I can hardly believe my luck!' One day, over
tea and homemade Battenberg cake, infused oddly and
slightly alarmingly with rum, he shared this thought with
her.

Tears glittered and swam in the old lady's eyes. She
leaned across to pick up one of the silver-framed photographs and stared at it for a little while, head on one side.
Placing it face down on her lap, she dabbed away the tears
with a hanky taken from her sleeve.

'Sorry, Gran,' said Jack, his own voice breaking a little. 'I
didn't mean to upset you.'

'Oh, good gracious, you didn't upset me, sweetheart,'
she replied, leaning forward to pat his knee gently. 'He's the
one who upset me, bless his selfish old heart, dying and
going off like that.'

'You still miss him?'

Alice sipped a little of her tea. Now there was a twinkle
in her eye. Young people did ask such extraordinarily silly
questions sometimes.

'He was very good in bed.'

Jack stared helplessly at the cake. Battenberg, infused or
plain, had never been so interesting. So colourful. So fasci-
natingly geometric.

She took pity on him.

'I'm sorry, Jack. I didn't just mean sex, although I do miss, you know, intimate closeness. No, I meant that he was literally good – a good person, even in bed.'

Her voice softened.

'They were the . . . the bookends in my life.'

'What were?'

'Kisses. Little kisses. He kissed me every morning just after we woke up, and he kissed me every night just before we went to sleep. Bookends. Keeping things safe and in their place. Every morning. Every night.' She leaned back in her chair. 'Can I tell you something about my husband, Jack?

The young man stirred uneasily. Alice chuckled, patting the photograph on her lap as though it might understand the joke.

'No, don't worry. I'll keep it clean, I promise. It's about something your grandad once said. It was about three months before he died, when he was already very ill. There was a nice man called Steve who was our neighbour when we lived in Nutley, just over the hill past the Indian restaurant. You wouldn't remember, but I think you might have actually met him once or twice. We still exchange Christmas cards. He was one of those wonderful paramedic people, like on the telly. Very kindly, when his shifts worked out right, he used to come in and chat with William after tea sometimes. One evening he was telling us that a checkout man had been rude to his wife in the supermarket that day.

'"I felt very cross, but I wasn't sure what I ought to do about it," he said. "Then I thought, William would know. So, suppose someone gave your Alice a hard time. How would you deal with it?"

'My poor dear husband was confined to a bed downstairs by then, and he could scarcely move, but – well, what can I say? It was a mini-resurrection. He grabbed the side-rails of the bed with both hands, sat himself up straight, hair all spiked out wilder than ever like one of those wind farm things, and barked, "What would I do? I'd find out where he lived, then I'd go round there, call him out to the pavement and punch him on the chin!"

'And I swear to you, Jack, he would have dragged himself out of that bed to do it. He was an old-fashioned man. A trusty knight. William was everything to me. Do I still miss him?' She gazed into the distance for a moment, hugging the photo against her chest beneath crossed arms. 'I ran out of luck, Jack – I ran out of luck.'

The only uneasiness between Jack and Alice had arisen from discussion, or rather lack of discussion, about his beliefs. It was unsettling and upsetting for Jack. He had never been very clear about Gran's views on such matters, but she was a supporting wall in his life. Her approval and encouragement had never failed to strengthen him. Added to this was a fear that she would miss out on an eternity of joy if she failed to grasp the truths that had become so much a part of him. He scratched the edges of this evangelistic eczema until it was sore.

It wasn't even that she argued against the things he said. She didn't. Nor did she laugh at any of his ideas and enthusiasms. In fact, it was her lack of response that he found most frustrating and bewildering. She just sat and looked at him with knitted brows. Puzzled concern. That was her expression on these occasions. One day he asked her to tell him honestly why she showed such scant reaction to the things he said about something that was so important to him. Alice shook her head and blinked apologetically, reminding Jack of Daphne from the *Eggheads* when an errant fact eluded her. She did give him an answer of sorts, though.

'You must forgive me, Jack, you really must. It's just that – well, when you talk about all those things, I promise I do listen very carefully to the words, but however hard I try, I can't seem to hear you saying anything . . .'

Jack was silenced by an inner breathlessness of hurt and bafflement. This was a frightening departure from the Jack-and-Gran norm. From that moment conversation on the subject languished and died. This unique failure in their relationship hung around the room whenever they met from that day onwards, manifesting itself in a mutual shifting or evasion of eyes from time to time. It made little difference to their affection for each other, but it was definitely there. Alice and Jack never spoke about faith again. After the death of his grandmother, that unresolved issue was a stone in the shoe of Jack's recovery from the first moment of aching grief.

Alice left quite a lot of money to her only grandson. It would be helpful, a pillow perhaps on which to lay his head when nothing else worked. He wrote a cheque for a five-figure sum – ten per cent of the total amount – made out to his church, and dropped the envelope into the postbox round the corner from his house, dusting his hands dismissively on hearing it fall with a faint flapping noise into the darkness. 'That's got that done,' he muttered to himself as he turned and trudged away.

Alice also left her grandson a letter.

Jack took a week off from his job at the Church Centre in Bromley to organise the emptying of his grandmother's flat. It was his second experience of sorting through the possessions of someone he had loved very much. It was as distressing and hateful as the first. It was as though any reason for existence had departed from Gran's possessions in the same way that the soul had disappeared from her body. Ornaments, pictures and furniture hung or stood around looking blank and abandoned and horribly tidy. Like inhabitants of some inaccessible other world, Alice and her precious William peered out at him from the photographs on the bureau. Hopefully. They were together now, on the other side of that glass.

By the end of a dark and sweaty week, Jack's work was very nearly complete. Emotionally exhausted, he locked Alice's front door for the last time and laboured slowly back along the seafront and up the hill to his hotel just as darkness was beginning to fall. Way down below on his left the sea drove and sucked and drove again as it had always done. Two lines from a poem he had once heard looped round and round in his mind, easily eclipsing any trace of spiritual optimism after a week of such gloom-laden travail.

Every damn thing must be tutored by the sea
That rolls and rolls and rolls and never says a word to
    me.

It was a relief after turning off High Cliff into Mount Road to see the familiar welcoming frontage of the Hydro Hotel, Jack's favourite place in the world to stay. The Hydro was a solidly traditional Edwardian establishment graced with plushly furnished, high-ceilinged lobbies, its essential Englishness sustained very successfully, mainly by East Europeans nowadays, and none the worse for that, as far as he could tell. There had been no question of camping out in Gran's flat. The eloquent silence of that echoing space was almost terrifying.

After the evening meal Jack took himself to a table in the big conservatory overlooking the croquet court and the invisible ocean beyond, ordered a pot of the strongest coffee available, and took the envelope containing Alice's letter from his shoulder bag. He had been saving this moment until the decks were cleared, as it were. A chance to hear his grandmother's voice speak to him for the last time.

On the front of the envelope, in Alice's neat handwriting, were the words, 'For my darling Jack.' He opened it with a little breathy sigh, took out the folded sheets of writing paper, smoothed and flattened them on the table in front of him, and began to read.

Somewhere out in the darkness beyond the croquet court and the passing street and the lower main road and the promenade and the pebbled beach, the sea continued to roll.

3

The Letter

My dearest Jack,

Hello to you, my lovely grandson. In case you want to know, I am beginning this letter to you on the fold-down bureau in front of my lovely big window facing the ocean. The sun is shining (this town is reported to be just about the sunniest place in Britain, you know!), the sky is bluer than a hedge-sparrow's egg, and the sea is just lying back floating on itself, smugly beautiful, wearing its best diamonds.

I've been remembering when you were here to help celebrate my eighty-sixth birthday. We had one of our best times, didn't we? In the morning I generously let you push me all the way along the lower promenade to Holywell, which, as we discovered yet again, is always further than we think. We had a reasonable coffee there and we talked about political inertia and, much more importantly, the strange effect of seagull noises on the psyche. Remember? Then, after I went home for a bit of a sleep in the afternoon, you took me for an early evening dinner at my favourite Thai restaurant in the new Marina. I can't remember exactly what we ordered, except that I definitely had those delicious butterfly prawns that they do so well. My mouth is watering even as I write these words.

What did we do at the restaurant apart from eating? Oh yes. One of our most enjoyable hobbies. We tried to spot serial killers among the other diners, didn't we? There were one or two very strong candidates, I seem to recall, especially the man on his own at the next table but one. He was slumped in his chair with his lower jaw sticking out, swinging his big head from side to side like a turnip on a pole, with a grim, predatory look on his face. Staking out possible victims, we assumed. Then it all got spoiled when his pretty wife and two bright-faced children came in and he was magically transfig-ured into a lovely, cheery, kind person who told bad jokes, obviously much loved by his family. Terribly disappointing. Fancy spoiling our fun like that. Some people have no consideration for others, do they? Either look like a serial killer and be one, or work harder at projecting your more positive side. That's what I say.

We had a great time, Jack. You insisted on paying, and I am of course excellent company, so we were both happy.

There was only one moment when things went a bit wrong. Do you remember us drinking quite a cheerful toast to your mum and dad in Thai beer? That was fine, but then I said something without really thinking.

'Let's hope they're happy wherever they've ended up.'

Something like that. A dank and dreadful silence fell at that point, and it became quite uncomfortable. I knew why, of course. Neither of us are likely to forget that horrid sinkhole of a moment when you asked me why I never seemed very interested in the things you believe – your commitment to Christianity.

I *want to apologise for my lack of courage on that day, Jack. My reply to your question was pathetic, and it was only half true. I think I said something about not finding any substance in what you said or the way you talked, something like that. Ever since then, as you know, we have ducked our heads when anything remotely connected with the subject has arisen. It may have been quite a small elephant, but it was always lurking somewhere in the room, and, as you have probably realised, the paradox is that those creatures grow larger the less they are fed. I think we both heard the clump of heavy feet in the Thai place that evening. It made me feel very unhappy.*

This is going to be a longish letter, I'm afraid, but I need to write it for two reasons. One is to try to make up for being so unhelpful and cowardly. I want to finally explain what I meant when I offered you such an unsatisfactory reply. And the other reason, a very strange and singular one, you might feel, is born in something that has happened to me, an experience that I would never have expected. I am very bad with labels, and I really cannot find the words to explain what I am talking about at this moment, so I shall not try. Suffice it to say that it involved the nativity (for want of a better word) of something new, something that you might want to call faith, and that it was brought to me through the agency of the man I want to tell you about in this letter. It is in connection with him that I want to suggest something it might be good for you to do.

So, first of all, what did I mean about the way you spoke to me about your faith? Oh dear. This is not easy.

I'll just have to think it, feel it and then get it written down. Don't go away.

OK, I'm back. I've thought and felt, so there is only one part of the process left. Here goes. I had the distinct impression that when you talked in my direction about faith, I wasn't actually involved in the conversation. It seemed to me that you were talking to yourself rather than to me. You only wanted me on board so that I could somehow assist you in the primary task, which was to convince yourself that you believed what you were saying. I wasn't just confused. I felt worried as well. How had you got yourself locked into this tiny cell of fear and confusion where you had to rush madly around in a confined space, talking loudly about the need for others to enjoy the same freedom that you had found? None of it made any sense, but passion inspired by fear is almost impossible to argue with. I chickened out. I could have buckled down and thought it through and made an effort. I didn't and I'm sorry. I didn't want to run the risk of damaging – well, us. I wanted you and me to go on as we always had done. I hope you feel, as I do, dear Jack, that we have managed to do that by and large. But I know too well the shadow was there. Until now, I hope. I am truly sorry, Jack. Please forgive me.

And speaking of shadows brings me to that other reason for writing this letter. Let me tell you about something that happened to me last year. One or two bits of this tale are strange and quite embarrassing for me to reveal, and you will be only the second person to know my terrible secret. I'm afraid you might find it a little upsetting as well. Oh dear. I think I'll stop now, and start this bit tomorrow morning.

Here I am again. Breakfast is all cleared away, the sun is still beaming, and there's no excuse for putting it off. Here goes.

It was January. You know what January can do to you, Jack. It's a bit like those long-haul flights. I've only done one, when I went with William to visit his older brother in Australia. When we first boarded the Qantas plane at Gatwick Airport, I remember the side of the seat was gently touching my knee. Not uncomfortable, you understand. Just a very slight pressure. By the time we arrived at Changi Airport in Singapore for our four-hour 'break', that harmless bit of seat had become a red-hot metal spike boring into my leg as though it was drilling for oil. All I really remember of Changi, apart from its size, is the blissful sensation of freedom from that aggressive attack on my trapped body. Worse for William, of course. He was much taller and bigger than me. He hardly complained, though. Very annoying. He left it all to me. Selfish as ever.

Anyway, January, and this January in particular, was just like that. You know how much I loved your grand-father, and how difficult it was for me to face or even envisage a future without him. Grief is terrible, Jack. You have experienced it yourself, so I know that you understand. I think that we lived with our sorrow over your father's death in rather separate ways, but we were comfortable with each other in our silences as well as in the things we said. It was the right way for both of us, and we did all right. We survived somehow, didn't we?

But, you know, grief never goes away. I suppose we learn to steer our lives a bit better, just to get by, just to go and buy baked beans and a loaf of bread at the corner shop. But the huge monster with the sharp teeth is always waiting behind a tree or just round a corner, ready to jump out and grab us and remind us that, deep down, the pain is never really any less.

Having said that, at the end of December I was feeling quite pleased with myself. Instead of sitting at home and getting depressed through the Christmas holiday, I had made all sorts of constructive plans for visiting and being visited by people I liked (including you, Jack) and going to things that would involve dressing up and arranging transport and making a real effort. It seemed to be working quite well. But I made a mistake.

I actually went to an old folks' party at one of the Eastbourne Anglican churches in the middle of town on New Year's Eve, the worst night of the year for lots of people like me. It was as profoundly, embarrassingly dreadful as one might expect. Lots of coy tittering over half a glass of warm white wine, intense discussions about the state of our legs, a game of New Year bingo in which I won a woollen egg-cosy that wasn't quite finished, and a flurry of faux excitement at ten o'clock, the hour when the schedule demanded that we pretend it was midnight and kiss each other on the cheek. I don't know if you've ever seen elderly people kissing each other in those circumstances, Jack. Elderly person A holds elderly person B's head very carefully with both trembling hands in case the pressure of the bacon-rind kiss causes it to topple off and fall like one of those stone balls you see on the top of posh gateposts.

I know that sounds harsh. Nice people, and it was all very well meant, of course it was. But this particular distraction was a mistake, and such a failure. It fell like a leaden domino that, in the process of falling, knocked over all the little pillars of satisfaction I had managed to erect and arrange around the Christmas season. They can't have been very substantial in the first place, can they? Later that evening, sitting in the back of an expensive taxi on my way back to the flat, the pain of living without William knifed into me so mercilessly that I almost doubled over in my seat, and I could hardly breathe. The long-haul of my lonely life felt as if it would last for ever, and there was no reason to suppose I would ever land in a better place, or that the pain would get any better.

It didn't. Things got worse and worse as that dreary month rolled on. I got caught up in one of those circular things that you can't escape from. The more depressed I got, the less I wanted to see anyone I really cared about, and the less contact I had with people I loved, the lower I dangled over the pit, like that poor man in the Edgar Allan Poe story. Don't be cross, Jack. You are a sweet man, whatever you believe. I know full well you would have dropped everything and rushed down to see me if you'd known, but all my confidence had gone, you see. I was crouching miserably in a little dark world without William. That was all there was. That was all I was.

Jack, forgive me if this shocks and hurts you, but I decided I didn't want to be alive any more. I wasn't quite sure how I would end my life, but I was determined that I would make it happen soon. If there was the slightest chance of being reunited with my darling husband, then whatever the cost it would be worth doing. And if there was nothing on the other side of the grave it wouldn't really matter. The pain would stop at last, and the emptiness could swallow me up.

Then it happened.

It was a Thursday, and the weather that day had been the exact opposite of what I see through my window as I write this letter. Rain and wind had been battering the seafront since early morning. When I pulled back the curtain in my sitting room at six o'clock in the evening the sky was as black as the gap in my life, and great gouts of rain were being flung by the gale in huge handfuls down onto the pavement on the other side of the road. Apart from splintered beams from the odd car, the only lights I could see were the pretty pastel-coloured ones that had been set up along the promenade the previous year, and even those rigid fixtures seemed to be straining and quivering in the storm.

I decided to go out for a walk before suppertime. Why? Why did mad Alice do that? Don't ask. Just bonkers, I suppose. I remember hearing on the radio once about a tribe in Africa where the young men have to go through a long, tough initiation process before they can be regarded as adults. Someone asked a tribal elder why they needed to be put through all that pain and strain. His answer was so unexpected.

'If they didn't do that,' he said, 'they'd probably burn their villages down, just to feel the heat.'

Going out into the storm was a little like that, Jack. A great big roaring stimulus to fill a gaping vacuum. In any case, why not? There was nothing to fear. If I went down to the beach and a force ten wind picked me up and swept me into the Channel, I would feel nothing but gratitude. Being run over would have done just as well, as long as the vehicle was big enough and travelling at a good speed. I did dress for the weather, though. What would my mother have said if I hadn't put my waterproofs on? Don't laugh. Practical, trivial habits die awfully hard, and besides, I always hated upsetting my dear mother.

'Doing yourself in is one thing, Alice,' she might have said, 'but going out in bad weather without wrapping up properly is quite another.'

I managed to cross the road without causing distress to traffic, and then I fought my way along the promenade and, with quite a lot of difficulty because of my stupid legs, down to the old Victorian bandstand that has always been one of my favourite places to be when a storm is blowing. On the side of the circular bandstand nearest to the sea was a sturdy wooden shelter facing out towards the ocean. I was fairly sure that the bench inside was set back far enough for its occupants to find respite from the roughest weather. Buffeted and soaked, I was still pinching the sides of my rainhood over my face as I gasped my way into the shelter and slumped, dripping and dishevelled, onto the bench as heavily as a featherweight like me is able to slump. I *pulled the hood back onto my shoulders, blinked the moisture out of my eyes and gave my hair a shake. In the process I happened to glance to my left and suddenly became aware that there was a darker patch of shadow at the far side of the shelter. I was not alone. It gave me such a jump. I think I gasped quite loudly.*

There was a man sitting on the other end of the bench.

Human beings are strange creatures, aren't they, Jack? This one is, anyway. The idea of being swept out to sea or run over by a bus or shovelling tablets into myself until I drifted into unconsciousness and death – those all seemed quite acceptable as means of flicking the pain switch to 'off'. But finding myself unexpectedly alone with a strange man on a stormy night in a place where no other person was likely to turn up was abso-lutely terrifying. I was planning to top myself, for good-ness' sake. Being murdered by someone else had not been a feature of the brainstorming process, not even a little scribbled note on the bottom right-hand corner of the flipchart.

I thought about leaving – quickly. I didn't, for three reasons. First, I couldn't. I haven't been able to move quickly for years. Second, if I did move, it could precipi-tate something. He might jump to his feet and grab me. Those who claim that women routinely fantasise about rape have obviously never had access to the inside of my head. My third thought was that this man, whoever he was (and all I could see of him was a sort of man-shaped silhouette), must surely have assumed that soli-tude was guaranteed in a beach shelter in the centre of a

crashing storm in the middle of January in Eastbourne.
I was the one who had turned up. I was the intruder.
Nevertheless, I was seriously frightened, so frightened
that I defaulted to being very English.

'Good evening,' I said politely, raising my voice
against the wind-fuelled cacophony outside, and doing
my best to steady the tremor in my voice. 'I do hope I'm
not disturbing you.'

He turned his head slowly to look in my direction
when I said that, and although I couldn't detect any
specific detail of his face, from that moment the fear
began to fade. I have no idea why. All I can say is that
the fringe of hair around his head was . . . it was a good
shape. I know you'll be laughing at me now, Jack. Well,
laugh away, but it was. It was an exceedingly good
shape.

'Not at all,' he said. 'It's a pleasure to have some
company. Always good to share a decent storm.'

His voice, Jack. Rich, warm, reassuring. The voice of
a mature man, I guessed. Mid-sixties perhaps. I've
always had a bit of a thing about voices. William had a
lovely voice, except when he got cross and barked. This
man's voice invited me to belong. It suggested that I
already belonged. We were Community. Sound ridicu-
lous? It is. But we were. How do you create that with a
handful of words? I sigh as I write.

'Are you a local person?' I asked.

'Actually no,' he replied. 'I'm lucky enough to have a
cottage in the country, a couple of miles from
Wadhurst, more or less between Hastings and
Tunbridge Wells. You?'

'Well, I – look, do you mind if I move a little closer so I don't have to shout?'

'I'll move.'

That might have been a little worrying, mightn't it, Jack? But it wasn't. He shuffled a few feet closer, leaned back on the bench and stretched his legs out in front of him.

'Better?'

'Much better. Thank you. I've got a flat just over the road and along a bit. It's what they call a garden flat. Tiny garden. No stairs. I can walk a bit. I made a huge effort clambering down here just now. But up and down's not very good for me.'

He nodded slowly, but didn't say anything else. I decided I would.

'So are you here in Eastbourne on business, or . . . or visiting someone?'

'No, neither of those. I'm on holiday, as a matter of fact.' He gestured over his shoulder with one arm. 'A week at the Sheldon in Burlington Place. Nice breakfast. They cook it as though they're planning to eat it themselves. And, crucially, good coffee.'

I considered this.

'You take your holidays in January in Eastbourne? Do you have family or friends down here?'

He chuckled softly.

'No, none of those either – except you, I hope. You seem nice. Never really been to Eastbourne before. As for taking my holiday in January. Hmm, well, I suppose I do like a bit of bleak. Something to do with how I grew up, I suppose. We all miss the rotten stuff from *time to time. Nostalgia, is it? No, more than that. Touching base, perhaps? Whatever it is, winter by the seaside fits the bill pretty well, don't you think? Mind you, I'm a lousy cheat. I'm only into bleak part time. The Sheldon's cosy and warm and the towels are fluffy. Lots of piping hot water. Worth coming out into a storm just for the pleasure of going back.'*

'So Eastbourne was just a random choice then, was it?'

'Random? Not at all, no. A friend recommended it. My friend George. He spends time down here.'

He seemed to be studying my face in the darkness for a moment.

'Tell me something about you. What you said is right. Winter holidays at the seaside are a little odd, but not quite as strange as what you've just done. What was important enough to make you battle your way down here on a wild day like this? You could easily have come a cropper on those two sets of killer steps up there. No one would have known. I'm glad you did roll up, it's a pleasure to meet you, but there must have been some very good reason for an expedition like this.'

I lost it a bit then, Jack. I was gobsmacked, or whatever the fragrant modern expression is. I didn't know how to answer his question, so I lied. I said the thing I wished was true.

'I don't know really. I've been shut away inside all day. I fancied a bit of a blow before supper, so I left my husband there to put the final touches to the meal, and just – came out. He said I shouldn't go, but I'm afraid I'm very stubborn. I hadn't realised just

*how bad it was, so when I got opposite the bandstand
I decided to come in here out of the rain and wind
for a few minutes before going back. Speaking of
which . . .' I raised my left wrist and did some ludi-
crous peering in the direction of a non-existent
watch. 'I need to get back. William will be wondering
where I've got to.'*

'William.'

'William's my husband.'

*'I think the wind's dropped a bit. Do you want to
take my arm and I'll give you a hand back up to the
road?'*

*'Oh. Oh. Yes. Thank you. Yes. Thank you very
much . . .'*

'May I ask your name?'

'I'm Alice. What are you called?'

'Doc. You can call me Doc.'

Jack laid the sheet of A4 paper down beside his coffee cup
and scrubbed his face with his hands. A few moments
needed to process feelings and information. Alice's
attempted explanation of her attitude to his faith had
shaken him. What was it she'd written?

'You are a sweet man, whatever you believe . . .'

What did that mean? How could that make sense?

But the news that his grandmother had wanted to end
her life and, for whatever reason, had failed to call on
him for help cut very deep, and was frightening on some
fundamental level. Jack had never had to deal with the
silent, inescapable message of that act. Now, though, he
sensed it.

'You people who care about us. You family and friends and lovers who hold us in your hearts. You are not enough. If you were enough, we would stay. We are leaving, and you will only discover we have left by accident.'

It was a harsh logic.

Jack whispered into his cupped hands, 'Oh, Gran! I don't think you ever realised how much I needed you to need me. I should have told you. And you should have told me. You really should have told me . . .'

He glanced again at the sheet of paper in front of him. Clearly the whole suicide thing had passed. Gran had died a natural death. He knew that. But what was all this about an experience of something-you-might-want-to-call-faith, and a strange man encountered in the middle of a storm? And, he asked himself as he picked up Alice's letter once more, what on earth was the thing she wanted to suggest that might be good for him to do?

The mind boggled. His grandmother's ideas rarely ran in straight lines, to say the least.

Pocketing his key and gathering together the envelope and sheets of paper, Jack settled his bill at the bar and retired to his room on the third floor. Here, in the uncluttered privacy that only a double-locked hotel room can offer, he took a whisky from the mini-bar and settled himself by the window that commanded a 'side view of the sea'. This facility added ten pounds to the nightly rate but, as far as Jack was concerned, was worth every penny. In this comfortable eyrie he felt paradoxically closer to the dark, pounding sea and the desolate beach, and lost souls like himself, and the looming mass of Beachy Head in the far distance to the west.

He picked up his grandmother's letter and continued to read.

So off we went, Jack, me all bundled up again, and he with the collar of his coat turned up round his face, and I must say, it was so good to have a strong arm to lean on. William would have approved. Not of me going down to the front on my own. That would have made him cross. But accepting help from a gentleman – he would have seen that as good common sense.

We said nothing to each other as we made our way up the steps and across King's Parade onto the opposite pavement. No point. The rain wasn't quite as bad as it had been, but the wind was thrashing everything in sight like a mad person who felt he was about to be frustrated. It wasn't until we were under cover in that little white-painted portico outside my flat that we were able to hear ourselves speak. I could see him more clearly now by the light that hangs above my door. I'd got the age about right, I think. He had a fine face. Clean shaven. Good looking, but not like a film star. More like a stage actor. A creased face, lots of lines, but all interesting. Eyes sad but kind. A hard-won joy in there somewhere perhaps, if that means anything. Brown, wavy hair, slightly long for his age, invaded by grey, beaten into curls by the wind and rain. He looked so safe, standing there with his hands thrust down into the pockets of his Barbour coat, waiting, I assumed, for me to disappear into my flat and close the door securely behind me. I had started to say something very

predictable about appreciating his help, when he inter-
rupted me.

'Alice,' he said, 'I would love to meet William if that
was possible.'

My Yale key was actually in the lock when he spoke
those words. I froze. There was no William. William was
dead. I had lied to this man who called himself Doc.

Never mind. A quick excuse. Dinner as good as
ready. Another time perhaps. So good of you to walk
me back. That sort of thing.

'Yes, that would be lovely. Come in and meet
William. There's plenty of food for two.'

A few minutes later, with our wettest things depos-
ited in the hall, I showed him into the sitting room and
invited him to sit in the larger armchair, the one under-
neath that print of mine that you like so much. The one
called 'Pals', with two men sitting side by side looking a
little nervous, but willing to be painted. Of course,
you've inherited that by now, haven't you, Jack? How
lovely to think of a picture William dearly loved hang-
ing on one of the walls in your home.

I'm wittering on because I'm embarrassed about the
thing I'm going to tell you now. I want to describe
what my visitor would have seen as he sat in that chair
and looked around. At the end of the room furthest
from the window, my gate-leg table, the one where you
and I sometimes sat, was set up for supper. There were
two places laid. Two mats, two wine glasses, two
tumblers, two side plates and two embroidered servi-
ettes rolled up in my mother's special silver holders.
Standing on the place mat furthest from the kitchen

hatch was a photograph facing across the table. It was a full-face portrait of William, taken a few years before his death. Just before he set off to town to get that photo taken we were laughing because I had asked him to pretend that he was smiling at me when the photographer pressed his button, and I truly think he did. Everything that my husband meant to me was in that picture.

All through that wretched January I had got into the habit of laying up the table for William and me every evening. I chatted to him through the hatch as I got the meal ready, and then talked to him as I ate my food, and enjoyed him being there opposite, smiling at me and listening. What a very sad person you must think me, Jack. A silly old biddy playing games like a child to fill up the gap in her life.

I think my visitor realised what was going on straightaway. I had a feeling he knew even before he came through my front door. He just sat in his chair for a couple of minutes with his chin resting on his interlocked fingers, waiting for me to say something. I felt like a very little girl, standing there by the table, nervously pitter-pattering one of my hands rapidly against the other.

'William died a long time ago,' I stuttered at last. 'There's only me here.'

He nodded and smiled and said very gently, 'I sort of thought that might be the case, Alice.'

'What gave me away?'

He smiled ruefully. 'Not very clever detective work, I'm afraid. You said there was plenty of food for two. So . . .'

'*Oh my goodness, yes, how silly.*'

'*More difficult to understand, Alice, is why you asked me in at all.*'

Jack, do you know what I mean when I say that sometimes you have to take a moment to sift right down into yourself to discover the bedrock truth, even if it turns out to be something you don't really want to say out loud? That's what I had to do when he asked me that question.

'*Well – look, I really don't want you to misunderstand what I'm going to say now – er, did you say I should call you Doc?*'

'*Yes, Doc's good.*'

'*OK. Well, the thing is – Doc – that although I only met you half an hour ago, I want . . . I want you to believe that I'm a person who will tell you the truth. I know my short track record is not very good. I started very badly down there on the beach, but I wanted to, you know, make it all right. Oh dear, does that sound very stupid? After all, there's no reason why you should . . .*'

'*What are we having for supper, Alice?*'

My brain double-declutched. (You won't know what that means, but I can't be bothered to explain.)

'*What? Oh, yes, of course. Would cheese on toast with bacon on top be OK?*'

'*Wonderful.*'

'*Good, I'll just, er, clear William away, shall I?*'

We both smiled when I said that. It was like a little bubble bursting. Through the hatch, and as we ate at my little table, I babbled on and on about my life, my marriage, you, my chronic loneliness and, finally, when we were settled in comfortable chairs, nibbling choco-late straws and drinking some rather inspiring Ethiopian coffee, I told him about my decision to kill myself.

'Having you here has been a lovely, unexpected treat for me,' I said, 'but tomorrow is coming, and the day after that, and the day after that, and on and on, maybe for years. Hundreds of tomorrows. People live for so long now. I don't want all those days. I don't want to wake up every morning with pain filling me even before John Humphrys gets into gear.'

I glanced apologetically at William's picture. 'In the end, you don't get a lot back from a photograph. As far as I can see there are only two choices. Stay and suffer, or make a decision to step voluntarily into the darkness, wherever that step might take me. And it's not a neurotic issue. I'm not clinically depressed and I think my marbles are all intact. It's about being practical. And I have made my practical choice. Do you think it's the right one, Doc?'

He sipped his coffee thoughtfully, rather as if he was being asked to decide between Crunchy Nut Cornflakes and Weetabix. He looked so nice sitting there, Jack. Nice clothes, expensive, but tough and durable. Dark brown trousers made out of some corduroy material, a thick-knit, dark blue pullover that had probably come from the same shop as that green coat with the check lining now hanging on a peg in my little hall. The shoes he had slipped off and left on the mat as we came in, I'd noticed were made out of chunky brown leather, heavily laced and built for use rather than ornament. I liked his clothes.

What would he say now in answer to my question? It was unfair, really. What could the poor man say? Sensible advice about broadening my perspective, getting out and joining things? Therapy? Counselling? Medication? Looking forward to springtime and the better weather? Asking myself how people who loved me would deal with the terrible news of my death? One or more of those, I guessed.

Doc finished a chocolate straw and set his cup and saucer down carefully on the little side table next to his chair.

'Alice,' he said seriously, 'I think you have made the right decision.'

Why do we tilt our heads and poke them forwards when we are surprised and puzzled? So undignified when you catch yourself doing it. I must have looked like a startled tortoise.

'I'm sorry, are you saying that you think I should kill myself?'

He tucked his elbows in against his ribs, and raised and lowered his hands in parallel with each other, as though he was balancing an argument.

'Of the two options you mentioned, that's definitely the one I would go for. Living the rest of your life in misery, or taking one simple step to make it all go away – well, there's no contest, is there? That's what I think.'

We sat without speaking for a few moments after that. I felt as if something had ended badly. Coldly. Just one comfortable platitude, surely?

Doc broke the silence.

'Alice, there is one other alternative that you may not have considered.'

Back on track. I breathed in through my nose with relief, preparing myself to be kind but dismissive.

'And what is that?'

Pause.

'Scrabble.'

It was like hearing the punchline of an incredibly funny joke. I burst into uncontrollable laughter and continued to laugh in a way that I hadn't done since before William's death. Partly a nervous reaction, I suppose, but it was more than that. The tears of mirth that filled my eyes that evening must have had some kind of cleaning agent in them. That's how it felt. People talk about falling about laughing, don't they? I ended up leaning over the side of my chair with a handkerchief stuffed into my mouth, trying to get a grip. So undignified.

When I'd calmed down a bit, I apologised, but Doc just smiled and said, 'So – what do you think about the Scrabble option?'

'I'm sorry, I don't know what you mean. Are you saying that I should join a Scrabble club or something?'

The smile dropped from his face and his eyebrows shot up in alarm.

'Good God, no, you've already lost the will to live. Why make it worse? No, I'm just suggesting that you and I having a game of Scrabble this evening is an option you might add to the miserable life and painless extinction choices. What do you think?'

I felt lost but oddly happy. 'Doc, what you're saying doesn't make any sense at all.'

'Well, no, it doesn't, but shall we have a game of Scrabble anyway? I love it. I should warn you, though. I am so good.'

'So am I. All right, let's have a game, but what makes you so sure I've got a Scrabble set, or that I might be keen on playing?'

'Oh, yet more great detective work. I can see it on the shelf at the bottom of your bureau. There are no other games there, so I'm guessing that when you moved to your flat you had to downsize, so you dumped any other board games you had, but you hung on to Scrabble because you love it and hoped you might be able to have a game sometime.'

'All right, Sherlock, you get the set out and I'll clear the rest of the table. I'll make some more coffee as well. But be afraid. Be very afraid.'

Oh, Jack, sweetheart, I did enjoy that game of Scrabble. Being with a warm, lovely, slightly edgy man, playing a game I've always loved. There was a glow around it all. And there was a new excitement in me, relief really, to discover that the mechanism for laughing like a drain was still there inside my tummy somewhere. I thought it was gone. Finding I'd still got it shocked me in a positive way. I certainly didn't call it the beginning of hope at that time, but I think that is what it might have been.

I nearly won the Scrabble, by the way. Let me bore you with the details. I lie awake some nights, just relishing the process by which I arrived at my final word.

Right at the end I needed a hundred and twenty-four points to win, and it looked hopeless. The seven letters on my rack were f, c, u, r, m, l and another u. Doc's last word had been 'spas', and it ended on the square immediately next to the red triple word square in the middle of the right-hand side of the board. If I could make a word that would fit on to the end of 'spas', I knew I'd get a very good score. It didn't look likely with my awkward collection of letters, but then I suddenly realised that they made the word 'fulcrum'. Wonderful!

But the question was, could any of those letters make a new word with 'spas'? I almost missed it, but it was there. The word was 'spasm'. That was my linking word, so I scored twenty-seven for 'spasm', forty-five for 'fulcrum', and, glory of glories, an extra fifty for using all my letters! One hundred and twenty-two points for one go. Not quite enough to win, but so exhilarating! And a record score for me.

Doc left soon after we finished our game. When he was all dressed up and standing in the doorway ready to face the weather again, he turned and said to me, 'Alice, I really enjoyed our evening together, and especially the Scrabble. I may be down in Eastbourne again from time to time. When I am, would it be OK if I gave you a call to organise another game? Obviously, if your answer-phone message says you've killed yourself, we'll have to give it a miss, but – well, it would be nice.'

I wrote my number on a sheet of paper from that little notebook of mine that lives on the hall table, and he dropped it into a side pocket.

'Thanks, Alice. Bye.'

That was it. He was gone. And so, believe it or not, was the sharp edge of my intention to kill myself. Don't ask me why. It just was. Weird. Something in me was lifted up. That's the nearest I can get to it. Apart from anything else, I've been less stubborn about letting people help me. As you know, those lovely people from Golden Hands come in every day now. Two of them, and the girl called Barbara especially, have become real friends. And Doc has been back. Two or three times since that first evening. He phoned me on each occasion, said he was in Eastbourne and asked if I would still be alive by the time he came round. So funny. Lovely times. Lovely conversations. Lots of buried treasure. And by going through that treasure I've learned some things I never knew before. You would be amazed. I won't bother you with those now. I'll tell you another time.

One other thing. The last time Doc came, he handed me a card just before leaving.

'A thought, Alice,' he said. 'There's a number written on here. It's not my direct number, but the person on the other end knows how to get hold of me. We've talked a lot about your grandson. If you ever think it might be a good idea for him to get in touch – well, he's welcome to call.'

So I've done that. You'll find the card he gave me in the envelope with this letter. Why am I leaving it until now? I don't know. Why might it be good for you? No idea. I'm just going with the flow. It's up to you.

Two last questions you may be aching to ask. Why did I never tell you about Doc? I suppose it's because meeting him was a little special nuggety thing just for me. I never expected to have another special thing in my life. I wanted it to be private. Mine. I have enjoyed writing about it, though. I hope you don't mind too much.

The other question is one I have often asked myself. It's about his name. What kind of doctor is he? Is he any kind of doctor at all? I still haven't got round to asking. I might have done by the time you get this, but I won't be able to tell you then. Take a look at that card. You'll be none the wiser. I wasn't.

That's about it then, Jack. I'll stop my rambling. You may not get this letter until after I've gone. Remember that I shall love you always.

From your adoring Gran xxxx

P.S. I said I would tell you what happened to me another time, but that may never happen. If and when you meet Doc, ask him to fill you in on the big change that dropped into my life. He'll know what you mean.

Jack laid down the last sheet of Alice's letter and glanced at his watch. It was late, and the inside of his head felt quite badly bruised. Not a good time to tackle the job of teasing apart the strands of confusion and childlike alienation that were knotting his emotions. He decided to block it all out temporarily by watching an episode of *Miranda* on his laptop. Better than an aspirin. After that, sleep, or lack of it, would have to look after itself.

One thing before that, though. Taking the envelope that had contained Gran's letter, he stood up, squeezed the sides at the bottom, and shook it over his bed. An olive-coloured card fluttered down onto the quilt. He picked it up and squinted at it under the bedside light nearest to the window. There were two lines printed on the card. One gave a telephone number. The other consisted of three words: 'THE SHADOW DOCTOR'.

4

Contact

Finally deciding to make contact with the person who called himself the Shadow Doctor was a nightmare process for Jack. How would he even begin his conversation with this man who had recommended his number be passed on to someone he had never met? The grandson of a friend. How strange was that? What could it possibly mean? What if, horror of horrors, the whole thing turned out to be some kind of massive scam? He dismissed the notion almost immediately. Gran might have been a little vulnerable in her loneliness, but she was nobody's fool. If Alice Merton believed in the man she knew as Doc, then he must surely be OK, trustworthy at least. And if, as Jack was conjecturing and hoping, this was to be another step on his spiritual pathway, why not just get on with it?

Such an easy question to ask. Sometimes, as he lay in bed nervously rehearsing various sets of words that he might use in that nerve-racking telephone call, he deliberately interrupted himself by concentrating on a mental picture of the candle flame that had flickered so nervously and uniquely in Ripon Cathedral on that distant rainy day. Something had to happen. Things were getting worse. He was turning into a husk of himself. All that he heard and saw seemed to be forced through a monochrome filter. Colours and shapes were losing their distinctness. Dullness reigned. A false identity was still better than no identity at all, but it was becoming harder and harder to maintain. Deep in his heart Jack knew that his future depended on fulfilling a desperate need to become more authentic as a human being. He also knew that it would not be easy. He had default settings for just about every aspect of Christian living and thinking. Some of those voices might have to be silenced or muted. Could he do that? How could he do that? And anyway, God might not exist at all. In which case none of it mattered. Jack stirred himself to bat that thought away each time it entered his head. How could God rescue him if he didn't exist?

In the end the nightmare was transfigured. After a difficult start, it became a very different kind of dream. Dry mouthed and apprehensive, Jack finally made himself ring the number printed on the olive-coloured card that had been lying safely in a desk drawer during the weeks since his arrival home from the Hydro Hotel the day after reading his gran's letter. Someone answered almost immediately. It was a woman's voice, warm, modulated and welcoming.

'Hello, Martha here. Thank you for calling. What can I do to help?'

The female voice was a small shock.

'Hello – yes, I'm not sure if I've got this right, but I was told that I would be able to contact someone called . . .' Jack pretended to read the name on the card. 'Someone called . . . I think it says "The Shadow Doctor"?'

'Yes! Spot on.' She sounded delighted.

'I think he – the Shadow Doctor, I mean – knew my grandmother, Alice Merton.'

'Good heavens! Jack! You must be Jack Merton! Doc will be so pleased that you've got in touch.'

'Oh. Good. Er, I wondered if I could speak to him.'

'Of course! But he doesn't live here, Jack. No problem. I'll give him a call straightaway and he'll get back to you as soon as he possibly can. I know he'll be so pleased.'

'OK. Thanks, Martha. Thanks very much.'

'Thank *you*, Jack. So lovely to meet you. Bye!'

Jack stared at the phone in his hand. He felt slightly dazed. His brief conversation with the lovely Martha had been like a sudden dip into a warm, bubbly bath. Perhaps being famous felt a bit like that. Something approaching adulation from people who have never met you. Who was Martha? What was her connection with the Shadow Doctor? All very puzzling.

He made a cafetière of coffee and sat by the kitchen table, sipping from his favourite fine-china, powder-blue mug and waiting for the phone to ring. Silly really. It could be hours or even a day or two before the mystery man called.

It was five minutes. So disconcerted was Jack by the half-expected sound that he fumbled with the mobile phone as he grabbed for it, and had to juggle furiously to prevent it dropping to the tiled floor. What a way to start. Thank God for invisibility. He controlled his voice carefully as he spoke.

'Hello, Jack Merton here. Can I help you?'

'Jack. It's Doc. Your gran's friend. You got in touch. I'm so pleased.'

The voice was rich and engaging, to Jack's ears, layered with experience and possibilities.

'Hi. So that would be Doc, short for Shadow Doctor, would it?'

'Exactly.'

'Thanks for calling back, Doc. Gran – Alice – left me a long letter about all sorts of things, including how she got to know you. She passed your number to me and suggested I get in touch. I'm not sure why, but I know you and she became good friends, so I thought it might be good to just touch base and . . . well, touch base.'

Jack had run out of harmless things to say. Hope had rather abruptly caught up with reality. Perhaps it really was just a matter of touching base. He was on the cusp of sinking to a depth of disappointment that surprised him. There was a short silence before the Shadow Doctor spoke again.

'Alice loved you more than anyone else in the world, Jack. You must be missing her terribly.'

The words came out before Jack could stop them.

'There's no one else I can talk to.'

But it transpired that there was. The dam may not have burst, but it certainly cracked. Later, unable to remember all that he had said to Doc in the course of that call about his life, his faith and his fears, Jack reflected on Alice's comment about the way in which the same man had succeeded in creating a community of two within minutes or even seconds of their first meeting. After nearly thirty minutes of laying his soul bare he began to understand, but how had this unusual man managed to do it on the phone?

Eventually, exhausted and slightly embarrassed by his own outpourings, Jack fell silent.

The Shadow Doctor broke the silence. 'Jack, thanks so much for talking to me. You asked me just now why I was hoping you would get in touch. There is something I would really like to ask you about. I wonder if you might be able to visit me at home. I gather you tend to be busy at week-ends. How about a weekday evening? You're in Bromley, aren't you? I live in a cottage on the edge of a forest down in Sussex, about a mile out of Wadhurst. What would that be – about thirty-five miles? Where I am is a bit remote. Stay the night. We'll make an evening of it. I think it could be important – for both of us. If you're up for it, I'll give you my direct mobile number, and you let me know when you can make it.'

Community or no community, fear burned suddenly in the young man's heart. Fear of the unknown. Fear of losing control. Fear of a dark place on a dark night. Fear of a strange man. Fear of his own fragility. But retreat was not an option. Ahead, that tiny flame burned less intensely but more manageably than his fear. So many questions. One very important one rose to the surface of his mind. What would Gran say? He did at least know the answer to that. Just do it.

'OK, Doc. A bit scary, but I would like to come. I'll save your number if this is the one you mean, and call you soon. And . . . thanks for letting me talk.'

'My pleasure, Jack, I'll look forward to hearing from you.'

And that, bewilderingly, was that. Two days later a date was chosen and agreed. Arrangements were made. An address and directions were supplied. Only one thing remained. Jack had to turn up. Two weeks later, on a Wednesday, Jack left work early, grabbed a bacon sandwich and a coffee from Greggs, and joined the daily procession of vehicles inching their way towards the main road. He knew the basic route well from his excursions to see Gran.

A21, an excruciating bit of M25, back onto the A21, head for Hastings, then out through Lamberhurst and into the village of Wadhurst. A mile after that, according to his instructions, he would see a sign on the left indicating Northfields Road. Three quarters of a mile down that lane he would see the words 'Marlpit Cottage' on a wooden sign nailed to an ancient oak tree at the start of a rough track running between two cultivated fields.

Jack's route planner had suggested that the journey would take a little over an hour, but the southbound traffic at every slip road and junction had seemed more grindingly bovine than ever. It was dark and just beginning to rain by the time he had driven through Wadhurst and spotted the sign for Northfields Road just in time to avoid overshooting it. After that the narrow country lane twisted and turned so frequently that it was difficult enough to avoid running into the hedge on at least two occasions, let alone estimate whether he had travelled less or more than a mile. A growing panic was relieved by the sight of what looked like a flashlight being held at head height on the left-hand side of the road, rain flashing across the beam like needles of light. Behind this full-moon effect a massive, dark shape rising high against the paler darkness of the sky could, he decided, only be a tree of some kind.

'An oak tree,' whispered Jack tensely to himself, as he pulled up in front of the gently waving light. 'Please be an oak tree.'

Seconds later the light was swung downwards and the silhouette of a man appeared outside the passenger window, making wind-down motions with his upraised hand. Jack lowered the window and leaned across.

'I really hope you're the Shadow Doctor,' he called plaintively. 'It's getting a bit dark and difficult along here.'

'Yes, I'm Doc,' said the man. 'It's not brilliant out here either. Well done, Jack, you're all but home. Listen, I'm going to trot back up towards the house and guide you in with the light. This is a very unlit part of the world. When you get up to the end I'll point you to a space on the right. My big old car is parked in there. Stick yours on the left of that. It'll be fine for the night. I'm getting wet. I'll see you up there.'

As Jack turned carefully onto the uneven track that gave access to Marlpit Cottage, an exquisite and totally unexpected peace fell upon him. A sort of freedom. Strange. At first he assumed that it must simply be the relief of reaching his destination, but there was something much more than that. It was as though a deeply buried memory of how it felt to be truly alive was surfacing in him for the first time in years. Doc had said he was all but home. That was how it felt. Memories of visiting his grandmother as a little boy filled his mind. Uncomplicated pleasure. A guarantee of welcome. Unconditional love. Something like that. A sort of freedom.

Guided by the light from Doc's swinging torch, Jack parked safely in his allotted space, picked up his bag from the passenger seat and stepped out of the car. It was too dark to see much, but the sound of his own car door slamming seemed inordinately loud as it picked up echoes from the surrounding area. Gazing into pitch darkness behind the gabled cottage, he could almost believe that the trees of the forest were registering his arrival.

'Follow me, Jack.'

Slinging his bag over his shoulder, Jack followed the Shadow Doctor across a paved area and waited as his host unlocked the front door of the house and reached around the door frame. Light streamed across the yard.

'Come in – you're very welcome.'

Jack stepped across the threshold.

5

Learning to Fly

The fire had settled down by now. No roar. Few actual flames. A glowing, pulsating heat transforming the dimly lit sitting room into something like a cave. A haven in the wild wood. Outside, on three sides of the cottage, endless cohorts of trees shared their defence of the sweetly seductive, terrifying darkness that is peculiar to ancient English woodland.

'Safety,' whispered Jack to himself – surprised, almost shocked, by this unexpected reminder of how it felt to surrender. He nearly cried. All that struggling. All the time. All those feverish boxing matches in his head. No winners or losers, just endless dodging and punching and being punched, and battling to remain upright. Now this. An actual experience of peace, the greatest prize that he could imagine.

It was the first time in his life that a decanter of whisky and a tumbler had been placed carefully at his elbow without invitation or comment. He dared to pour himself a half inch of the golden liquid, removing and replacing the glass stopper of the decanter with meticulous care. His host might regard clinking and clattering as evidence of vulgar haste. He cursed himself as that thought entered his head. This fragile surrender of his was more likely to be shattered by guilt than by noise. Idiot! You don't deserve peace. Drink your whisky.

Jack knew that bad whisky has no real confidence. It wastes its brassy effects the moment it enters your mouth. All flare and no substance. Not this one. This filthy, bog-strained, peaty Scotch slipped with deceptively mild ease along the length of his tongue, blossoming into his throat with something approaching a benevolent triumph. It was simply magnificent. Unworthy, Jack sighed and turned to his host, who had re-entered the room and was seated comfortably on the other side of the fire, a dark chalice of red wine balanced between the finger and thumb of his right hand.

'If you don't mind me asking – how did you know I enjoy whisky?'

The Shadow Doctor studied the glowing ruby depths of his wine seriously for a moment, then turned towards Jack, his satchel of a face crinkling into the whimsical, prophetic smile of Paul Schofield's Thomas More.

'I certainly don't mind you asking, Jack. But, to be honest, I didn't know for sure. Instinct, I suppose. When it comes to the truly serious things of life you can usually rely on instinct. I certainly wouldn't have wasted a single drop of that heavenly elixir on anyone who wasn't likely to enjoy it.' He extended a hand in Jack's direction and continued reverentially, 'That, my friend, is a sixteen-year-old Lagavulin, produced, appropriately, I'm sure you'd agree, in Lagavulin Bay. Some say it works like a depth charge. What's your opinion of it?'

'It works like a depth charge,' agreed Jack, nodding and peering into his glass as he mentally computed the cost of that half inch of fine whisky. He seemed to recall that aged Lagavulin retailed for sixty or seventy pounds a bottle. He had only ever gazed on it from cyber-distance afar with sad, sober eyes.

'Is there really a place called Lagavulin Bay?'

'You may have to die before you're allowed to see it, Jack, but I know it exists. I was given a few bottles by a friend who works up there in the distillery. Good man. Very generous. A couple of cases. And they arrived just as twilight was falling on a November evening. Autumn gold to the power of ten . . .'

'A couple of cases? You must have done something amazing for him.'

'Oh, I wish, Jack. No, I just gave him a hand when he needed to clear a little space last year. He told me he gives loads of stuff away to cover up the fact that he's stingy. Christian, do you think?'

Jack released a little explosion of laughter.

The Shadow Doctor smiled appreciatively.

'I like you, Jack. You can come back and drink my whisky any time. You're completely right, of course. There can be a very thin line between cheerful obedience and some bone-aching struggle to pretend we're better than we are.'

And getting thinner by the moment, thought Jack. He stared into the fire, his whole body tensing with the effort it would take to release words that were already shaping his lips.

'As I said to you on the phone the other day, I've always struggled. Always.'

The other man nodded his head slowly, but said nothing.

Whether it was the early effects of the Lagavulin or the Holy Spirit, Jack neither knew nor cared very much at the moment. He also knew almost nothing about the faith or lack of faith of the man sitting opposite him. That didn't matter either. All he knew for sure was that the heady cocktail of freedom and safety was opening him up in a quite unprecedented way.

'I've tried so hard. I really have. I've wanted the things I believe to be true and all right and everything people said they would be, but I'm beginning to feel like someone who's ended up in the sea after a plane crash. That's never happened to me, but I've often tried to imagine what it must be like. You've got your feeble torch going and you've blown your little whistle over and over again, but it doesn't work. No one comes. It sounds OK when they're doing the safety talk before take-off, with the lights on and the stewards all smart and confident, and sounding as if one of the main problems would be making sure women take off their high-heeled shoes before they slide elegantly down the escape ramps. But think how different it must be when you're lost in the night in the cold and dark, and the waves are high, and none of the stuff they gave you works or makes any difference, and your breathing's gone all wrong, and you know you can't stay afloat much longer. Horrible. Lonely. No one comes. I've felt like that.'

Jack put his glass down beside the decanter and placed his steepled hands against his face. The Shadow Doctor seemed to understand.

'I do know, Jack,' he said quietly, 'that there are times when the signposts to truth and betrayal seem to lead in exactly the same direction. But . . .' He glanced around the room. 'I think – I believe – that this is a safe place. You can take risks. You can say dangerous things if you want. Tell me anything. Tell me that the phantom of C.S. Lewis, ruddy-faced as ever, pops into your place for a pint every Thursday evening. Tell me you're a rapist or a bank robber. Tell me you're a rapacious, bank-robbing paedophile. Tell me that you've decided to embrace the medieval heresy of Modalism. If you're in particularly advanced confessional mode, tell me you're a member of UKIP. Tell me you're a saint. Tell me you're an agent of Satan. Tell me the truth – about you.'

Jack lowered his hands and sat back in his chair, eyes wide open, suddenly overcome by the peculiar draining fatigue that often accompanies emotionally weighty decisions. On a shelf at the other side of the room a large model of a hare, fashioned out of something that looked like bronze, stared at him with outraged, toothy contempt.

'I've never shared it, that feeling of being completely lost. I told you on the phone that Dad and Gran are the only people I ever shared anything with. As far as stuff about faith is concerned, I've never shared anything much with anyone. Not real or important things, anyway. Until now I've never been the person who goes on about no one coming. I haven't dared. I'm the exact opposite. I help. I rationalise. I found a role. I've become the one who sorts things out. I'm the Jonty Rhodes of our Christian community.'

He glanced at the Shadow Doctor enquiringly. Doc nodded. 'Great South African cricketer. Genius fielder.'

'I'm like him,' Jack went on. 'Not the genius bit. I mean that I dive and stretch full length to catch other people's doubts and fears and frustrations before they can do any real damage. I never really solve any of those problems. I just move them around in my hands. I reshape them. I throw a different light on them.'

'You . . . transform them into a virtue?'

'In a way, yes. Can you imagine? That's precisely what I do. Ridiculous, isn't it? What a clown I am. Yes, I transform them into a virtue. People come knocking on my door with their begging bowls, and I'm neurotically driven to fill them with little crumbs of hope.'

Doc held up a hand, fingers spread wide like a fence, and smiled. 'I'm choking on the metaphors, Jack. Tell me something. Does this ever actually help people? Do they go away feeling better?'

'It looks as if it helps. I mean, the ones who come to me with their upsets and problems usually say how grateful they are, but . . .'

'But you don't get many miles to the gallon with solutions like that?'

Jack stared at him. Like many clever young men, he was not always quick to see a simple meaning in what others said.

'Oh, I see. Yes. I mean . . . no, you're absolutely right.' He continued glumly. 'The same ones tend to come back pretty regularly with slightly different versions of whatever was troubling them the last time. There's no real change.'

The Shadow Doctor quoted softly:

I sing my insecurity with confidence,
My melody is music to their ears,
A symphony of light, on the verge of endless night,
A lullaby to charm and calm their fears.
Have mercy, Lord, have mercy on your servant,

Dusk falls and I am weary to the core,
I beg you, find some peace for me, let someone else
    agree,
To stand up on a platform and be sure.

For at least a minute only two sounds could be heard – a
sudden intensely industrious crackling from the fire, and
the occasional rattle of raindrops on glass as a south-west
wind gusted against the windows on the west side of the
house.

'And why do you do it, Jack?'

Jack looked into his tumbler and saw that it was empty.
His hand strayed towards the decanter. He drew it back
again, raised his head and turned towards the other man.

'Do you think it would matter if I had another whisky?'

The Shadow Doctor sighed, shaking his head rapidly
from side to side. Moving out of his chair and down onto
one knee, he took a while lugging a birch log from the
bottom of the wood basket next to the hearth before throwing it expertly to the rear of the firebox. Levering himself
back into his seat, he closed his eyes and repeated Jack's
question.

'Would it matter if you had another whisky? Let me see.
Yes. Yes. It's coming through loud and clear. Bad news. One
more Scotch and it's the white-hot tridents for you, my boy.
Fight the temptation and you might have a slim chance of
making it through the pearly gates.'

'I only meant . . .'

'For God's sake, Jack. For his blessed sake and mine,
please don't ask me or him for permission to have a second
tot of whisky. I cannot think of anything more ghastly than

the idea that some kind of devilish, synthetic morality should be allowed to smooth the rough edges of real life. Pour yourself another drink, or don't pour yourself another drink, or drink the whole damn decanter, and tell me why you go on trying to persuade people that black is white, and that white is actually a rather tedious shade of grey.'

He paused, then went on more gently. 'OK, perhaps I can get you started. It's not about them, is it? It's about you. You don't really do it for others. You want to be a kind man, but you actually do it for yourself, don't you? So, why not forget about that long queue of troubled individuals for just a moment and tell me why you find yourself incapable of allowing other people to suffer.'

Jack was confused. He felt as if he was being bullied by someone who was supposed to be on his side. He also knew that the next time he spoke he would cry. He just would. It was like standing on the edge of a cliff and wrestling with the mad, dreadful temptation to take one step forward into oblivion. He seemed to have lost shape in his mind, his spirit, even his body. His fingers. He clumsily poured another three or four pounds-worth of Scotch into his glass, but left it untasted beside the decanter as he tried to control his emotions.

'It's because . . .'

He took a deep breath.

'It's because . . . if I can't find a way of solving their problems, I haven't the ghost of a chance with my own. It's all chaos after that. It terrifies me. I know that if I ever let all that stuff get right inside me, I would have to face . . .'

'You would have to face your disappointment.' The Shadow Doctor's voice was quiet and very kind as he continued. 'The terrible "D" word. It's one of the saddest sounds in the world, isn't it? My goodness, you haven't enjoyed this blessed faith of yours for a very long time, have you, Jack?'

Jack shook his head, unable to control the trembling of his mouth or the emergence of a warm tear that trickled slowly down his cheek. Don't say anything else. Please don't say anything else.

'It's about that man, isn't it? Jesus. That would be my guess. It's about the difference between how you thought it would be knowing him, and how it actually is.'

When, later, he looked back on that strange evening when every familiar fence and boundary seemed to be fading and falling in the half-light, Jack especially recalled the dreamlike sensation of sharing his consciousness with the deep, warm rumble of the Shadow Doctor's voice, as that voice inexorably anatomised his own sadness and pain.

'Let me guess. You wanted him to be the best friend you ever had. The one who doesn't laugh when you say something silly. The one who never bullies. The one who knows you have your limitations, and accepts them for as long as it takes for change to happen. You expected him to be the one who is happy to wait, and pretend he's doing something else while you collect yourself, the one who needs you as much as you need him, the one who has defended you to the death and will happily go on doing that until you die. You knew that he is continually deserted, and because of that you wanted him to be the one who understands, who walks away beside you with his arm round your shoulders when the others don't want to know, the one who loves his friends and never, ever abandons them.'

Jack had to lean forward to catch the words as Doc continued. It was almost as though the man was talking to himself.

'The one who can imagine miracles so clearly that they become reality. The one who sees a little girl alive and well and needing her breakfast when everyone else says that she's dead. The one who would allow the same kind of miracle to happen for others through you, because you are his brother and his friend, and because he said clearly that his followers would do even greater things than he had done. The one who, at the very least, makes a bit of an effort to turn up from time to time.'

He turned to Jack suddenly. 'Something along those lines, is it?'

Jack took a sip from his glass. This time the blossoming glow seemed to flower up instead of down. Something heavenly in his brain.

'I know it sounds pathetic, but I feel deep-down guilty about the very idea of agreeing with you. I've spent so much of my time searching for good reasons why it doesn't work out the way it's meant to. Everyone, including me, seems to have a good stock of reasons – or excuses. I remember hearing a man on one of those Christian programmes that go on all through the night . . . have you ever watched any of those?'

The Shadow Doctor said seriously, 'I try to avoid pornography.'

Jack stared for a moment.

'Oh. Well, anyway, this man began his sermon or talk or whatever it was by saying that there are ten reasons why sick people don't get healed when they pray. Ten! It's the

56

same with me. Something I've done. Something I haven't done. Some prayer I should have said, but didn't. Something I've never understood about being a Christian. Some chronic sin that disqualifies me from having all the good feelings. It drives me mad, it really does. And the only relief from all that is when I manage to sort something out for someone else. Because, you see, I'm *testifying*. I'm *ministering*. I'm doing the Lord's work. All those words. All that stuff. It's like a bad drug. When I'm not doing it, I feel as if I don't really exist.'

He took another sip.

'But you're right. You are right. I do feel neglected and let down. And tired. I'm sick of it.'

The Shadow Doctor lowered a palm down on the arm of his chair in slow motion. 'No need to bother any more, then. Freedom at last.'

'What do you mean?'

He waved a casually dismissive hand. 'Well, you can give up all that faith nonsense now and get on with your life.'

Silence. Suddenly, despite the fire and the whisky, the room was far less cosy. Jack put down his glass and gazed wide-eyed into the depths of the fire. He felt little and frightened and lost.

'Truth,' said the Shadow Doctor reflectively, 'can be even more of a depth charge than Lagavulin, if that's possible, and it sometimes costs a great deal more than a bottle of good-quality Scotch.'

He quoted again:

Deep in winter sleep is where you hear the saddest
    cry,

The wheeling, dealing seagull souls
Of men and women taught to stay a step ahead
Who reached the edge
But found that when they fell
They had not learned to fly . . .

'The truth is supposed to set us free, according to someone who is widely held up to be uniquely qualified to comment in that area, but the fact is that lots of those who call themselves Christians simply cannot handle reality at all. Why would they want to? Facing the truth is a bit like jumping off a cliff. It can feel like the worst idea in the world. What would make you do such a thing when some sort of ghastly outer or inner death is bound to be the consequence? Why not stay on the cliff edge, or retreat and give up the whole idea of flying?

'You seem to be a good example of all that, Jack. Take this precarious faith or belief, or whatever you choose to call it, that has served you so poorly for so long. Do you think it had a gnat's chance of surviving some bulldozering truth that would crash through all the walls and defences and barriers and bars that have been erected to ensure that what we call the world of faith can be controlled and measured and understood by what a great poet once described as "twittering men engaged in inessential debate"? That's the same man, by the way, who also said, if I remember rightly, that it was "all rather pale and round-shouldered, the great Prince lying in prison . . ."'

He turned to face Jack, as though a new thought had occurred to him. 'Jack, do you fancy a spot of adventure – a bit of a risk? How does that sound to you?'

Jack's face was very troubled. His hands trembled slightly as they rested flat on his knees. He was the very picture of a young man who has no wish to go on an adventure.

'I'm not sure what you mean, and anyway . . . were you serious about what you said a moment ago, that I ought to give up, you know, being a Christian?'

'Well, I just meant that you might as well,' replied the older man evenly. 'It's clearly not doing you any good. All this strain and pain without any positive outcome. There's not a lot of point in suffering for the sake of it. Personally, I can't think of a more unpleasant, rancid dish than cold martyrdom. Besides, Christianity doesn't really work. I tried it years ago, and it nearly finished me off.'

Jack stared. 'So, you're not . . . sorry, from what my gran said in her letter, and after I'd spilled all that stuff on the phone and you said you'd like to see me, I . . . well, I suppose I assumed you were a . . . a follower of Jesus.'

'Ah.' The Shadow Doctor reached for a bottle on the floor beside his chair, poured himself some wine and stretched his legs luxuriously, holding his glass up so that he could enjoy the newly fuelled fire dancing in its depths. 'Now you're talking about something different – something very different. If you really mean it, that is.' There was a warning in his eyes. 'Even more frightening, perhaps. But very different. Jack, I told you that there was something I wanted to ask you about.'

For the first time Jack detected a hint of vulnerability in the Shadow Doctor's tone. A tinge of unease muddied the clean sheet of his new-found peace. He wanted Doc to be a mystery with a strong heart. At the moment weakness was likely to be infectious. On the other hand, if there was a possibility of change, he wanted it as he had never wanted anything before in his life.

'What do you want to ask me?'

A picture formed in Jack's mind of himself rising in the morning, gathering his stuff together, shoving it in his bag, throwing it into the car, driving his bumpy, disappointed way down the track to Northfields Road, and setting off on the dumbly inevitable route to a life that would remain unchanged for the foreseeable future. What did the Shadow Doctor want to ask him?

'I want to suggest that you come and work with me.'

The shock almost made Jack laugh. It was like sitting in a dentist's chair waiting for the pain to go away, and suddenly being invited to take over half of the practice. What did the suggestion even mean?

'I don't really understand. Are you offering me a job?'

The Shadow Doctor sighed. 'Not precisely, no, but something like that. Oh dear, I knew this would be difficult. As you may have noticed, I don't usually have any trouble wrapping things up in words, but this is really hard. Jack, I'm asking you to consider joining me in . . . in the things that I do, the contacts I have with people.'

'Like Gran was a contact, do you mean?'

The older man mimed reshaping an invisible substance with his hands. 'In a way, yes, but . . . no, it's more complicated and much less cold than that. Alice was my friend. I was very fond of her. Look, I think "contacts" was the wrong word. I would simply like you to join me in the life that I live. I cannot realistically continue on my own. I need someone like you, and I suspect that you might discover what you yearn for and have so far failed to achieve – when we are actually on the job, as it were.'

'On the job?'

The Shadow Doctor groaned, holding his hands up in surrender. 'Wrong again. Sorry. I suppose I'm talking about . . . doing it. Getting involved. Being in the flow.'

'But what is the flow? What do you do? What would we be doing?'

There was a hint of desperation in Jack's voice. At the moment all he could see was fog. Doc leaned his head back against his chair for a few moments. When he finally replied, his voice was calm and far more assured.

'I have been blessed and burdened with a responsibility for helping people with the shadows that blight their lives. At present I simply cannot deconstruct and explain the way in which that happens. I can, however, assure you that it does happen – not always, but often. My suggestion, Jack, is that you join me in carrying out this task. You and I would be partners, allies, colleagues. What can I offer you? Lots of things. Adventure. Hard work. Fascination. Great satisfaction. Disappointment sometimes. Impenetrable mystery. Occasional moments of sheer wonder. What do you think?'

'Are you talking about me coming to live here, in this house?'

'Yes. There are three bedrooms. Two quite big. I've got one, you can have the other one, the room at the front. You're in that one tonight. I use the single room as a sort of study. We can share that. Downstairs, this sitting room and the kitchen we came through, big enough to eat in. Internet works well. Will you come?'

One obvious, wide-eyed question.

'Doc, just tell me this. Why on earth would a man like you choose a person like me to help you with the sort of things you're talking about? I've already told you that my track record is dreadful as far as helping people is concerned. All patches and plasters. And you said yourself that I don't really do it for them at all. It's just a way of protecting myself from disappearing into the darkness. And you're right. I haven't got a clue. Basically, I'm a lonely, lost person who's useless at making friends. Why do you need me?'

The Shadow Doctor leaned across and laid a hand on the young man's arm for a moment before speaking.

'Jack, I don't retreat one jot from what I said to you, but nor do I turn a blind eye to my own stubborn refusal to engage with anyone who might question or comment on the way in which I handle my life. You have a very good, tender heart. I know that because of the way Alice spoke about you, and because I can see it for myself. Let me ask you this. Would you like to succeed in doing the very thing that has brought you to your knees?'

Something welled up in Jack's heart.

Tell him how you feel.

He almost choked on the words.

'More than anything else in the world.'

'I know. But you live on your own vastly underpopulated island. So do I. We run our inner worlds without constructive reference to anyone else. If you do decide to move in and work with me, I promise you that it will not be easy. I know that I am going to resist the intrusion into my space. Old habits die very hard, especially when they are born in pain. We are likely to fall out quite a lot in the early days.

But I can also promise you a rich and authentic involvement in . . . well, what I referred to earlier as "the flow". I'm not going to take that to pieces at the moment. I will work on that. It's a risk for both of us. Do you want to take it? Look, if it helps – how about coming for a couple of weeks? Make a decision after that.'

They sat without speaking for some time after that. Jack sipped his whisky. Doc played with the stem of his wine glass and stared into the fire.

'OK,' said Jack at last, hardly able to believe the words coming out of his own mouth, 'I'll come for a fortnight. Next month. Probably start on a Wednesday, to fit in with work.'

'OK,' said Doc.

6

The Black Plaster

On Friday night, the Shadow Doctor turned on the bottom stair as he was about to go up to bed and said, 'Oh, by the way, Jack, we've got someone coming to breakfast at half past nine tomorrow. He lives near Tunbridge Wells, his name is Daniel Tressingham, and he's being blackmailed.'

It was two days into Jack's trial fortnight, and the atmosphere in Marlpit Cottage was less than serene. The sense of profound peace that he had experienced during his first visit still tinged the air, but communication between the two men had been difficult, to say the least. An obscure unease was always going to prevent Jack from describing the initial encounter as a honeymoon period, but the magical essence of that original experience was significantly diluted.

It was not that Doc had been less than welcoming. The guest bedroom was clean and comfortable, the small bathroom at the end of the landing scrupulously organised and prepared for a second man's use. Jack, a keen, if hitherto rather solitary cook, was pleased to see that the fridge-freezer and the walk-in larder in the kitchen were well stocked. Clearly, a comprehensive shop had been done in readiness for his stay, and a couple of trips into the surrounding countryside in Doc's Nissan X-Trail had been pleasant enough, especially as it transpired that the Shadow Doctor was not at all keen on driving, while Jack had never enjoyed being driven.

'It's up to you,' Doc had announced during their first exploration of the narrow, winding lanes that seemed to lead invariably to a surprisingly vast reservoir at the bottom of the valley, 'but for the next two weeks – and for ever if you stay – you can do all the driving when we go out together. I'll put you on the insurance. I'm not interested in cars, but I love this one. I love being inside it. I am a bit of a small-world freak. I just wish it would leave me alone and let me think while it does its thing. I suspect it has to be controlled in the same way that you would control a difficult horse. Ridden rather than driven, if you know what I mean.'

Jack knew exactly what he meant by the latter comment, even if the rest was meaningless. He took great pleasure in sweeping the big silver car smoothly around corners, and gunning the powerful engine on straight stretches of road. It was as much as he could do to avoid making b-r-r-r-m, b-r-r-r-m noises as he drove.

It had all been very amiable and relaxed on the surface, and if the two of them had simply been on a little holiday it might have been fine.

It was not fine.

Doc appeared to have no specific agenda, other than a decision, or perhaps even a determination, to have no agenda. Questions nagged at the young man constantly. Why did Doc sidestep any discussion about what shadow-doctoring might actually involve? How were they supposed to organise this important time they were spending together? What was the reason for this clear but unexpressed ban on anything resembling spiritual conversation or activity, and, most important of all, when was something going to happen?

Any attempt to actually resolve these problems was met with deflection or flippancy or both. Jack detected a film of defensiveness lying across these responses, but Doc would not be drawn, other than to say that a clean sheet had been presented to both of them, and that scribbling impetuously on that virgin space would get them nowhere. Learning and development, he said, could only happen on the job.

'And,' asked Jack, 'when is that going to happen? When will there be a job for it to happen on?'

'Soon,' said the Shadow Doctor.

And that was all he would say.

His host's refusal to give any shape to proceedings had left the young man frustrated and slightly resentful. Now that it looked as if something was actually going to happen, he made a childishly conscious decision to withhold enthusiasm. A victim of blackmail was coming to breakfast. So what?

Jack placed a marker in his Michael Connelly paperback and closed it. 'Why breakfast?'

'I would hate you to think my life revolves around hard liquor, Jack, but I've been saving some particularly tasty whisky marmalade for a special occasion. Bacon sandwich, intoxicating marmalade, gallons of good coffee, fresh orange with the juicy bits left in – or added afterwards, who knows? Even blackmail won't seem quite so bad when he's faced with a breakfast like that, surely?'

'Does he know he's coming to breakfast?'

'Oddly enough, he does. Yes, of course he does. We're not going to ambush him with Shredded Wheat, entertaining though that sounds, now you mention it. I told him on the phone this morning.'

Jack tapped his book against the end of his chin, relishing a wodge of resistance in him to what he saw as Doc's whimsical, unconsidered approach to serious problems.

'If he's being blackmailed, he must have done something pretty bad. Do you really want him here at breakfast time before you even know what it was he did?'

The Shadow Doctor screwed his features into something like a fist, then lost control and laughed immoderately. 'Forgive me, Jack,' he said eventually. 'I have to confess that I'm lost when it comes to correct etiquette in these matters. Which meal do you think would be most suitable for a . . . what would be the term? A blackmailee? Lunch, perhaps? Afternoon tea? The threat of porridge? No, there are two things to bear in mind. One is that my friend George seems to think it would be a good idea for Daniel to come, and second, as one far wiser than I put it, blackmail is a black plaster on a black wound. No moral high ground available. Not for either party. Goodnight.'

Turning once more on the second step, he leaned the top half of his body back into the room and added provocatively, 'In any case, it's an excuse to start the marmalade. I only bought it to share with bad people. Saints like us would have had to wait.'

7

Breakfast

Jack woke early the following morning. He lay still in his bed for a few moments, conscious of a negative memory niggling at him like a bad taste from the night before. On the wall opposite hung a huge black-and-white print of the young Vanessa Redgrave. It was the first thing he saw in the morning. He had thought he might replace it if he decided to stay, but had changed his mind. She lifted one magnificent eyebrow suggestively at him now as he struggled to remember what was blighting his peace. Yes, of course. He groaned inwardly as he mentally replayed that last little bit of dialogue with Doc the night before. That was the niggle.

Why did he do that sort of thing? Why, over this short period, had he given in to a temptation to be combative with the older man, especially as Doc became such an annoyingly shifting target when Jack made any attempt to challenge or provoke him? Like some sort of benevolent matador, the Shadow Doctor seemed to have the knack of diverting attack with a single twitch of his verbal cape, leaving Jack bewildered and, paradoxically, relieved that no injury had been caused.

Jack was hazily aware that much of his frustration was triggered by a profound fear of operating without clear boundaries or processes. Unlike the Christians that Jack had known, the Shadow Doctor rarely offered any verbal clues to his spiritual perspective or state of mind – if he had one. It was almost as though he refused to be personally in charge of his own decisions and activities.

For some reason the memory of a brief conversation entered Jack's mind. It had been the only half-serious exchange between the two men since his arrival. It had been on the afternoon of the day he moved in, when nerves suddenly set in and any decision to alter his life so radically was beginning to look ominously as if it would be a dark and dreadful mistake.

'What should I do?' he had asked in that vulnerable moment, apropos of nothing at all, feeling like a small child even as the words came out of his mouth.

The Shadow Doctor appeared to take his words seriously, nodding thoughtfully as though he fully understood the importance of the question.

'What is written on your heart, Jack?' he asked at last.

The unexpected question, couched in words that were strikingly out of kilter with Doc's usual conversational style, took Jack by surprise. The small child in him replied before he could be extinguished.

'Lots and lots and lots of things,' he said, simply because it was true.

'Make some space,' said the Shadow Doctor. 'Tell you what – let's both make something. You make some space, and I'll make some toast.'

The ambition had been there since that moment, even if the space-clearing continued to be a substantial work in progress. Writing on his heart, furniture in his mind, however you liked to put it, some rearrangement or replacement was going to be necessary, but there was no plan, no spreadsheet and no book of rules. Scary.

Sitting up in bed and turning to glance out of his window, Jack saw that a sparkling spring day was successfully getting itself together. He smiled, remembering what Alice was likely to say on days like these.

'Enough blue sky to equip the entire male population of Utrecht with weekday trousers and a spare pair for Sundays.'

There had been no sounds from the rest of the house yet. Breakfast. Jack decided to get up and busy himself preparing breakfast for Daniel the blackmailee. That might make up a little for his sulky tone last night. Dressing quickly, he tiptoed downstairs to make a start.

He enjoyed his self-imposed task more than he had expected. The weather was mild enough for breakfast to be eaten out of doors, and it would be even warmer by the time their visitor arrived at nine-thirty. He dragged the circular garden table and chairs from the patch of grass next to the chicken run and managed to make it reasonably stable on the stone flags outside the front door of the cottage, using scraps of wood and folded cardboard to wedge two of the feet. The rest was easy. Satisfying, even.

By the time the Shadow Doctor appeared at the front door of the cottage, Jack had consciously posed himself on one of the chairs beside the table, sipping coffee and tapping his teeth with a pencil as he frowned over yesterday's untouched *Times* crossword.

'I really don't know how you do these things. "Unremitting supporting political party in need of a large workforce." Six letters, hyphen, nine letters.'

'Across or down?'

'Down. Does it matter?'

The Shadow Doctor raised his forearms vertically against the door frame and hung his head, staring at the ground for a moment before looking up at Jack.

'Labour intensive?'

Jack studied the clue again for a moment. His eyes popped open with surprise. 'How did you do that so quickly?'

'How did you do *this* so quickly?'

The young man looked around as if he had only just noticed the laden table. 'Oh, breakfast, you mean?' He waved a hand airily. 'Well, I happened to wake early, so I thought – you know, might as well get ahead of ourselves. The, er, bacon and stuff is all out ready. Bread's perched in the toaster ready to drop. Milk's in a jug in the fridge ready to come out.' He reached across the table with his forefinger to tap the top of a small glass jar adorned with a stylish label printed in Victorian script. 'Whisky marmalade in pride of place. Haven't tried it yet, though. I'm happy to wait until the bad person gets here. Coffee? I've only just pushed the whatsit down. Left it three and a half minutes.'

'Perfect.'

Pulling out another chair, the Shadow Doctor sat down and reached for the cafetière, shaking his head slowly as if in wonder.

'Thank you,' he said, his voice warm with delight. 'You have made the beginning of this day a very happy one for me. Not only have you done all the work, but you have also given me a crossword clue that I was able to solve, and, despite being a follower of Jesus, you are very nearly reconciled to the prospect of breakfast with a sinner. What more could anyone ask?'

The irony was not lost on Jack. Doc knew exactly why he had got up early to do the breakfast. It didn't matter. Despite everything, the Shadow Doctor's approval was almost as warming as the morning sunshine.

8

Daniel

The visitor rounded the bend in the farm track at exactly twenty-nine minutes past nine by Jack's watch. The slim figure of the hapless blackmailee looked nervous even in the distance, like a man who is retreating in his mind even as he is walking forwards with his feet. Jack thought it likely that he had been lingering uneasily round the corner out of sight until the precise hour of his breakfast appointment. No wonder if his nerves were jangled. He was about to confess to something serious enough to invite blackmail. Policeman and voyeur jostled for pole position in Jack as the man drew closer.

Their guest seemed surprised at the sight of the al fresco breakfast arrangement. Perhaps he had been expecting an office with a desk and two chairs, or possibly a counselling room statutorily equipped with just enough comfort to prevent loss of focus.

'Er, good morning,' he began worriedly, as he stepped tentatively onto the edge of the flagstones, like an actor without a script. 'My name is Daniel Tressingham. I have an appointment to see . . . to see . . .'

'Call me Doc,' said the Shadow Doctor, rising and extending a hand. 'Daniel, you are very, very welcome.' He lingered over the handshake for a moment. 'Daniel Tressingham. A most interesting name, if you don't mind me saying so. How impressively punctual you are. Do sit down and let me pour you some coffee. Do you take milk? Sugar?'

Daniel lowered himself slowly onto one of the garden chairs, depositing his black-and-red backpack on the flag-stone beside him.

'Oh, black, please. No sugar, thank you very much.'

He glanced across the table at Jack with as much of an implied question as politeness would allow.

'This is Jack,' said the Shadow Doctor. 'He is my good friend and he works with me.'

Daniel Tressingham was probably in his early forties, slim, neatly dressed in light pastel colours, and clean shaven. The Shadow Doctor remarked later that, although the troubled expression on Daniel's face must have been exac-erbated by the situation he found himself in, a frowning, slightly hurt bewilderment was more or less locked into his features. He refused the offer of food at first, but Doc's whimsical geniality gradually massaged him into a more relaxed state. Jack remembered what Gran had said in her letter about the Shadow Doctor's ability to create commu-nity with very few words. It was fascinating to watch. Kind of awesome. How would one ever learn to do that? He quite quickly found himself warming to their naturally self-effacing visitor. What dreadful thing could such a mild and retreating man have done to get himself into the clutches of a blackmailer?

Daniel finished the last corner of his second slice of toast and marmalade and wiped the corners of his mouth care-fully with a paper napkin. He cleared his throat and stared down at his plate for a moment before speaking.

'Lovely. Very nice. Thank you. Do you . . . do you think I should tell you about my situation now?'

The Shadow Doctor said, 'Daniel, you strike me as a man who might be keen on cryptic crosswords. I'll give you a clue and you see if you can solve it.'

Surprise and an unexpected light appeared in Daniel's eyes. 'Crosswords. Yes, I love crosswords. Which one do you do?'

'I have a not very successful shot at *The Times* sometimes,' replied Doc modestly. 'You?'

'Yes, yes, I like having a go at *The Times*. Don't do that well.'

'Well, this is a clue I made up myself. Tell me what you think of it, Daniel. The answer has five letters, and the clue is "Compassion makes me cry".'

Jack found the ensuing silence very strange. He seemed to perceive or imagine a buzzing energy in the atmosphere around the table as Daniel, his eyes truly clear for the first time since his arrival, allowed his mind to tackle the problem. His lips moved silently as he repeated the clue to himself once or twice. At last a genuine smile temporarily swept the trouble from his brow.

'Mercy. The answer is mercy.'

'So it is. Yes, so it is.'

The sun shone approvingly.

'Anagrams are fun, aren't they, Daniel?'

'Yes. Well, yes, they are . . . can be.'

A sudden and, to Jack, inexplicable hiatus was broken by the Shadow Doctor. 'I'm sorry, Daniel, I changed the subject. You were saying about your situation.'

The frown returned and deepened. 'Oh, yes. Yes, of course. I'm not quite sure where to start.'

He moved his plate to one side and rested both lightly clenched fists on the table in front of him.

'Right. I do know where to start.'

He raised one fist and gently lowered it again.

'My family is one of the most important things in my life. I'm married – to Kerry, and we have a fantastic, cuddly little girl called Izzie, short for Isobel. We've got a really nice first-floor flat in Broadwater Down, just off Frant Hill in Tunbridge Wells, not far from St Mark's Church. That's where we go. I love Kerry and Izzie more than I love myself, I think, although . . .' He swallowed, struggling to control his voice. 'Although that doesn't mean much at the moment, I'm afraid.'

He stared imploringly at the sky for a second.

'Anyway, a woman came to see me last week at work. I'm in Planning. Our offices are up at Hawkenbury, on the edge of the town out towards Pembury.' He made a twisting movement with a bent finger. 'They're near the bends where the young drivers go mad. She just turned up. No appointment or anything. Normally I wouldn't have seen her, but when I heard the name . . .'

'You knew who she was?'

Daniel nodded miserably in answer to Jack's question.

'Her name is Naomi. Naomi Strang. Kerry and I knew her when we were living in a flat in Leicester Street near Victoria Park in Leamington Spa, the town where we worked after we got married. All three of us were civil servants employed in the same big office block. Kerry and I got married in the June. That Christmas there was a works party. I went, but Kerry was . . . well, she was poorly.

'Later on that evening I stumbled – literally – into Naomi in the corridor down by the gym near where the toilets are, and we . . . we started kissing. We ended up on a pile of mats in the equipment room at the end of the exercise hall. We . . . you know, we made love.'

The Shadow Doctor lifted his eyebrows a couple of millimetres.

Apparently interpreting this as a question, Daniel shook his head dismally from side to side. 'No, you're right, that's not true. We didn't make love. We just . . . did it to each other. It was horrible. I felt sick with shame and fear afterwards.'

Doc broke the silence that followed Daniel's confession. 'Why didn't Kerry go to the party, Daniel?'

'I told you, she was poorly.'

'You love her very much. You wouldn't have gone if she was simply poorly. Why didn't Kerry go to the party?'

Daniel twitched with unhappiness and folded his arms tightly across his chest. 'She wasn't poorly. We had a big row. A terrible, terrible row. Really . . . upsetting. And I deliberately bought a can of that very strong Special Brew stuff at the corner shop and drank it before I even got to the party. A couple of mouthfuls made me giddy. I never was a drinker. Don't like it much. And then there was so much alcohol on the tables when I got there. I went a bit mad. Drank far too much far too quickly. Just chucked it down my throat. Stupid. It's no excuse, but I hardly knew what I was doing. I can't believe what I've done. Kerry and I are Christians. It means the world to us. It's always been at the centre of my . . . my everything. Now . . .'

'Daniel,' said the Shadow Doctor, 'it must have taken a lot of courage for you to tell us all this. Try not to lose your nerve now. The argument. What was it about?'

Our unhappy breakfast guest dropped his hands to his lap. He looked as if he might collapse and burst into tears at any moment. He took a deep breath.

'OK, I need to go back a bit. Kerry had been acting strangely since the summer. She was . . . not herself. It began in August. We rented a cottage in a little leafy village called Litlington down in East Sussex for our summer holiday. It was lovely. There was a sweet, dumpy little church on the edge of the village – we've always liked looking round old churches. And there was a place called The Exeat a couple of miles away. You can walk right out to the sea past these big silver loops in the river just before it turns into a proper estuary. We took our binoculars. We've got two pairs. One brilliant and one not too bad. Kerry always insists I use the good ones, but I do try to share – you know – using them. There were lots of wild birds and sheep and things down by the river. It was a fantastic area. Perfect place to stay. We were very happy there for the first two days.'

He continued, his voice vibrating with recalled hurt and puzzlement. 'Then, on the third day, we went for a walk up past the church and found a signpost to a village called Alfriston, so we thought we'd go. It was just wonderful. One of the prettiest villages we'd ever seen. Very old. Amazingly preserved. And a lovely spreading green right in front of St Andrew's, the parish church. They call it the Cathedral of the South Downs. It was . . . exquisite. We were so happy.'

Jack watched Daniel's fingers twisting and untwisting as he continued. 'We looked round a bit and decided to have lunch in a café called The Copper Kettle at the end of the High Street. It was quite crowded, but the food was good. I noticed Kerry didn't say much while we were in there having our meal, but I didn't give it a lot of thought at the time. Then afterwards, on our way back, when we were crossing a bridge just near the edge of the village, over a river called the Cuckmere, I think it is, she suddenly marched off really quickly ahead of me and disappeared behind the trees further along the path around a corner. I had no idea what was going on, but I was worried. It was so strange. She went off so abruptly. It made no sense. So I hurried after her, and just past the point where she'd disappeared – it happened.'

Daniel's face contorted with the pain of his memory.

'Kerry, my lovely, loving Kerry, launched herself from behind a tree at the side of the path and started screaming at the top of her voice, right into my face. It . . . it was like a horror film. She repeated over and over again that I didn't love her. I'd never loved her. I loved a woman in The Copper Kettle. I wanted to . . . have sex with her. She didn't use those words. Much worse ones. It was . . . dreadful.'

He seemed to suddenly wake up to what he was saying.

'I couldn't ever have imagined those words coming out of her mouth. It made it even more horrible. She said I'd put my hand on this woman's knee when I thought no one was looking. I'd secretly arranged to meet her there. Why didn't I go off and . . . have sex with the woman in The Copper Kettle, instead of hanging about with someone I only pretended to love? On and on and on she went. Just one long wild-eyed screaming rant. And then, just as suddenly as she'd started, she stopped, turned round and marched fiercely off again, along the path in the direction of Litlington.

'I went all limp. I felt physically weak after what had happened. None of it made any sense. I hadn't even noticed this woman. I loved Kerry. I didn't want anyone else. We were a couple. I wanted to spend the rest of my life with my wife. And like I said, I'd never heard her use language like that. It wasn't the way either of us ever talked.'

'So you followed Kerry back to the cottage?' asked Doc quietly.

'Eventually, yes. I was dreading seeing her again. But when I got there I called out quietly through the doorway, and there was no answer. I found her in bed, sleeping like a baby. And when she woke up she was just her normal self. She was Kerry again. When I asked her if she was still upset, she looked shocked and frightened, but she didn't seem to know what I was talking about. Said she must have got a bit tired and carried away. I knew it had to be much more than that, but it was such a relief! I know it was probably a mistake, but I was so thrilled to see her behaving normally that I just pushed it all on one side. Told her not to worry and did my best to pretend nothing had happened.'

'Until the next time.'

The Shadow Doctor was not asking a question.

'Yes, it happened again. Not during that holiday, but a week or two after we got back. The same sort of thing. In one of our local pubs this time. We were there with two friends. I was just about to throw a dart, badly as usual, when I suddenly heard that same screaming voice coming from right across the other end of the bar. All about me. All

82

on one note. She was standing rigid and upright by her chair looking like a mad woman. Her eyes were . . . they were blazing and empty all at the same time.'

A shiver passed through his whole body.

'Horrible! It was so horrible. I bustled her out to the car as quickly as I could, with her still screeching on and on about how disgusting I was, and how I spent my time plotting against her. All sorts of really *nasty* things. I can't begin to tell you what it was like being in that car. Trying to drive along with that . . . that face spitting poison at me while I tried to drive. It was hell. It was like being in some sort of furnace. And then, well, it was weird. Her head flopped back against the headrest and she fell fast asleep. Spark out. Just like that. When we got home, I pulled up outside our house and just sat for a while. Then I reached across and prodded her shoulder – gently, you know. She woke up straightaway and stretched her arms out and yawned, then she climbed out of the car, wrapped her arms round her body and stumbled into the house and straight up to bed. I followed her. She was unconscious. Asleep. She hadn't even undressed. She woke up in the morning as though nothing had happened. Just like the time before.'

Jack's normal flow of response was inevitably checked by the presence of the Shadow Doctor, but a rising impatience drove him into questioning Daniel Tressingham with a little more asperity than he intended.

'Surely you must have tackled her properly then, Daniel. I mean, it wasn't as if you'd done anything wrong, was it?'

Energy drained from Daniel's voice. He sounded small and sad.

'You don't understand. I've always done something wrong. All my life I have found myself accepting that if something goes pear-shaped it's almost certainly my fault. If that sort of thing's drummed into you over and over again when you're little, you don't just believe it, you know right down in your boots that it's true. As a young man I knew I'd never ever marry. How could I? I'd get it wrong and be bad at it and ruin everything. That's why it was so brilliant when I met Kerry and we fell in love and decided to get married – she proposed to me in the end, by the way. I couldn't believe it. It was like the sun coming out when you're lost in the middle of the night. This beautiful, funny, clever Irishwoman with lots of glorious black hair. She loved me and wanted to be with me for the rest of her life. Why? I used to look in the mirror and just laugh. It didn't make sense. But it was true.'

'The argument?'

Flicking a glance at the Shadow Doctor, Daniel nodded unhappily.

'It happened twice more. After the third time we went through our usual nothing's-really-happened routine, but I was upset and worried and I could tell Kerry was as well. I was terrified that everything was going to fall apart. Kerry refused point blank to see a doctor. Said she hadn't been sleeping properly and it was a . . . a passing phase.

'After it happened a fourth time, in Marks and Spencer's, of all places, just by the shelves where they do those ten-pound offers, with people clustered round picking out the best deals, I knew something had to happen. The next morning I told Kerry I was sorry for anything I'd done to make things worse, but we couldn't carry on like this. After we get home today, I said, before we go to the works party, we're going to sit down together and decide what to do.'

He smiled wryly.

'She agreed. Probably the first time I've laid the law down since we met. We hardly spoke until we'd finished eating that evening, then we went into the sitting room and sat down. She burst into tears. Floods of tears. Told me she had a secret. Before I ever knew her, she said, while she was still living in Ireland, she'd had serious mental health issues. Psychotic episodes. A schizophreniform disorder was what it was actually called. They put her on medication and arranged some counselling. It all helped. By the time she came over to England, all the symptoms had disappeared, and her psychiatrist told her that moving in itself would probably help. Lots of her troubles had roots in the past – her childhood in Connemara. She'd decided to draw a line under it and hope she'd be able to get on with her life.

'She said that when we started to get close, and marriage was, you know, on the cards, she kept thinking she ought to tell me about her past. Knew she should. Nearly did lots of times, but never actually managed it. Too frightened. She was as bad as me. Always thought marriage was for other people. For sane people. Terrified that I'd dump her if I knew. Why would I want to be lumbered with a mad woman?'

'How did you react to all this?' asked the Shadow Doctor.

'I listened. Didn't move. I could feel myself not moving. Didn't say anything for a long time. Just sat and stared at her.'

'How did you feel?'

'I don't want to say.'

'Yes, you do.'

Daniel pushed his voice out through rigidly immobile jaw muscles.

'I was so angry! I've never been very good at being cross with anyone, but something went off bang in me. This person whom I'd loved and trusted and let into the very middle of me – how could she have let me go through all that? How could she have kept such a big, big thing to herself? I'm ashamed to say it now, but I left her crying on the sofa, pulled my coat off the peg by the front door and stomped off up the road. Stopped off for the Special Brew stuff at the corner, then went to the party and . . . well, I told you what happened there.

'When I got home . . . oh, it was so sad. Kerry was sitting on the sofa, just where I'd left her. I knelt down in front of her and she slid down on her knees, and we just stayed there crying together for ages. The thing is, we're through all that now. We both said sorry loads of times, and Kerry promised to go back to the doctor and get things sorted out. And she has. It's gone really, really well. Our doctor found exactly the right person for Kerry, and she's worked hard to take advantage of all the help she can get. Takes all her tablets and everything. Never misses an appointment with this lady called Ruth. Talks to me about how she's feeling. We're in it together now, and Izzie's come along. Our little miracle. We're as happy – actually, we're happier than we were before, but . . .'

'But you never did tell Kerry what happened with Naomi at the party.'

'No,' said Daniel quietly, 'I never did. Partly because I was ashamed, but just as much because I couldn't bear the thought of Kerry having to know what happened that night.

She would think it was her fault. She would be devastated. It was so grubby, and so . . . nothing. I know lots of men say that, but it was true. I was going to tell her because I didn't . . . don't want us to have any secrets, but I kept putting it off. I tried to tell myself that she'd kept a secret from me, so I could do the same to her. Ridiculous. But I'd almost managed to shut it away in a corner of my mind. Then, last week . . .'

'Naomi Strang turned up.'

'She said she'd got a cheap train ticket so that she could come to see me. She's going back to Leamington later today, but only if I meet her this afternoon in Tunbridge Wells and give her this.'

He reached down to his backpack and pulled out a sealed envelope, fatly stuffed with something. It dropped to the table with a dull thump.

'One thousand pounds in twenty-pound notes.'

The Shadow Doctor nodded.

'Presumably this is in exchange for her keeping quiet about what happened at the party.'

'That's right. When she came to see me at the Land Registry she asked if I remembered what happened at the works party. All sugary and coy, she was. It made me feel sick. Then she asked me if I'd ever told Kerry.'

He bowed his head and rested it on his hand for a moment.

'I should have lied. If only I'd lied. But I didn't. I went on and on about how hurt Kerry would be, and I begged Naomi to go on keeping it to herself. I was in tears. Naomi said I mustn't worry, because she wasn't going to say a word to Kerry. As long as I met her at one-thirty in Hoopers on

Saturday afternoon – that's today – with a thousand pounds in twenty-pound notes. The other thing she wanted was this. I have to sign it and give it to her with the money.'

From the top pocket of his shirt he drew a sheet of paper, unfolded it and slid it across the table to Jack. It was a dated statement with a space at the bottom for a signature. Jack read it aloud.

To whom it may concern,

On this, the above date, I have willingly and voluntarily repaid a loan of one thousand pounds to my friend Naomi Strang, with gratitude for her patience and generosity.

Daniel sighed. 'She didn't listen to anything I said after that. Just stared at me with a horrible, confident smile on her face. In the end I agreed, just to make her go away. As she stood up, her phone rang and she stepped outside to take it. I don't think she realised that I could hear her end of the conversation. She cackled with laughter and said, "Yes, my darling. All well. And I was right. A double whammy! Bye for now." After she said that, I could even hear the bloke on the other end of the phone laughing like a drain as well. She was going to get what she wanted, you see. The money and the signed statement about the imaginary loan. Then she went. And here I am.'

'How did you hear about Doc – the Shadow Doctor?' asked Jack.

'We were on holiday in Scotland last year. A man tucked a card into my top pocket as we came out of church on the

Sunday. I hung on to it because it seemed so quaint – odd. This week, when I'd run out of ideas, I . . . well, I just thought it might be worth a try. Kerry's having her hair done this morning, so I said I was going out for a drive – to enjoy the nice morning.'

Daniel looked at the Shadow Doctor like a hungry but not very hopeful spaniel. 'What should I do?'

Platitudes fluttered through Jack's mind, a flock of boring grey butterflies. Confess. Repent. Pray. Stand up to the devil. He determined to keep his mouth shut and wait. Doc might be whimsical and bewildering in his approach to problems, but Jack felt confident that he would do something.

The Shadow Doctor spoke at last. 'Hooper's. That's a department store, isn't it?'

'Yes, just opposite the station. Used to be called Weekes in the old days. There's a restaurant up on the top floor.'

'Was it Naomi's idea to meet there, or yours?'

'Mine. I don't think she knows Tunbridge Wells.'

'And what is Kerry likely to do after having her hair done?'

Daniel thought for a moment.

'Well, usually she'd meet her friend Janet for a coffee at Brown's in the Pantiles. That's why I suggested Hooper's, because it's way up at the other end of town. The last thing I want is for them to meet.'

'What time is her hair appointment?'

'Half-past ten, I think. Why on earth do you want to know that?'

Good point, thought Jack, why does he? Still, at least it would postpone the moment when Daniel had to trail miserably off to lay a black plaster on this reopened wound of his.

'One more question, Daniel.'

'Yes?'

The Shadow Doctor looked earnestly into Daniel's eyes. 'Is there a branch of the Halifax Building Society in Tunbridge Wells?'

Daniel seemed to shrink visibly. The faint light of hope in his eyes faded altogether. 'Yes, there's a branch up at the top of town just by the end of Monson Road. I use it myself.'

'Good! I need to get some cash. Daniel, I seem to remember there's a car park just on the edge of Calverley Grounds. You know it? Good. We'll meet you there and go for a walk together. Hang on while Jack and I clear some of this away, then we'll get going.'

9

Tunbridge Wells

Jack hardly spoke as he drove Doc's X-Trail north towards Tunbridge Wells. As they passed through the village of Frant he said boldly, 'I do hope you know what you're doing.'

The Shadow Doctor said nothing, but he did nod thoughtfully. There was no further conversation until they arrived at the car park in Tunbridge Wells twenty-five minutes later to find Daniel waiting miserably on the pavement opposite the Central Railway Station.

'Where are we going?' he asked wearily. He pointed up the hill. 'The Halifax is that way.'

'Plenty of time for that later,' said the Shadow Doctor carelessly. 'Let's take a walk down through the High Street. I haven't been that way for ages.'

He took the lead, setting off across Grove Road brightly enough, but Jack and Daniel trudged along side by side behind him, their glumness reflected by a sky that had faded from vivid blue to angry grey in the course of the journey from Wadhurst to Tunbridge Wells. Jack felt embarrassed and deeply troubled all over again about his rash decision to link fortunes with the Shadow Doctor. Liberation of the spirit was one thing, randomness under a dark sky on a failed and inexplicable mission was quite another. This was not learning on the job. As far as he could see, it was not anything.

So wrapped up was Jack in unhappy reflection that the trio had passed through Chapel Place and crossed the lower end of Frant Road into the Pantiles Walk before he suddenly realised that he was walking on his own. Turning, he saw that Daniel had stopped a few yards behind and was pointing over Jack's shoulder towards the Shadow Doctor, who could be seen standing at the top of a flight of steps, apparently staring through the plate-glass window of some kind of bar or café.

'It's Brown's,' said Daniel, catching Jack up and twitching worriedly beside him. 'Kerry will probably be there by now. I don't want to see her at the moment.'

But the Shadow Doctor was beckoning.

'Look,' he said, as the other two joined him. He pointed through the window towards a table set near the back of the bar. 'Lots of glorious black hair, you said, didn't you, Daniel? Is that Kerry in the red jacket?'

Daniel nodded, but his brow was contracting with puzzlement.

'And the woman with her – is that Janet?'

'No,' Daniel replied, his lips quivering with uncertainty and apprehension. 'That's not Janet. That's Naomi.'

'Ah,' said the Shadow Doctor. 'I thought it might be. I think you'd better go and join them, Daniel. I suspect you'll be able to save yourself two thousand pounds. We'd better get to the bank. Here, take this. My private number. Call later and let me know how it goes.'

10

Questions and Answers

Doc refused to say any more to Jack about what had happened until later that evening. After dinner the two men had steadily reduced a wedge of apricot cheddar until only the polite fragment remained. Daniel Tressingham called as Jack was debating whether to be sensible or generous. By the time the call ended and the phone was back in its cradle, Jack had transferred the tiny triangle of cheese to the other man's plate. Doc smiled at Jack and popped it into his mouth.

'Fascinating,' he mused, 'how, between us, we managed to reduce that large triangle of cheese to a miniscule but exact copy of its original self. You have your own very special way with a sandwich as well, don't you, Jack? I've noticed how you eat from one corner of a triangular sandwich at a time, so that what you end up with is a sort of precisely shaped arrowhead made of sandwich. Fascinating.'

'Riveting,' said Jack. 'Are you going to tell me about it or not?'

'About Daniel, you mean? Yes, it all seems to have worked out quite well. Naomi has gone home to her disappointed partner, having wasted the cost of a cheap train journey, and Kerry and her husband are safely tucked up with each other and little Izzie back in leafy Tunbridge Wells.'

Jack adopted the squarely symmetrical pose of one who is determined to stay rooted in his chair until all is clear.

'All right, let's go back to the beginning. Something I've been wanting to ask you all day. How could you possibly have known that Daniel was keen on doing cryptic crosswords? Did he have a copy of *The Times* poking out of his bag or something?'

Doc shook his head. 'Oh no, it wasn't that. I suppose the whole business of crosswords was in my mind after you had mentioned one of yesterday's clues before breakfast, and that is important, but something quite different gave me the hint.'

Jack raised both hands and turned his face away. 'Hold on. Before you tell me about that, why was me giving you a crossword clue before breakfast important when you met Daniel later on?'

The Shadow Doctor gazed up at the ceiling for a few moments. When he spoke at last, it seemed to Jack that he was struggling to describe something that he might never have put into words before. 'I suppose . . . well, I suppose I mean that any and every trickle could possibly, a bit later on, turn into the beginnings of what I have previously referred to as a "flow", and if it really is a proper – a useful – flow, then, well, you might want to go with it.'

'You might want to go with the flow?'

'Yes.'

'And that's important.'

'That might be very important.'

Jack leaned back in his chair and nodded sagely. 'So, assuming that I've understood what you mean by that, now tell me how the crossword trickle turned into a crossword flow after Daniel arrived. What was this hint you were telling me about?'

'It was his name.'

'His name? Daniel Tressingham, you mean?'

'Yes, doesn't that name strike you as being just a little odd?'

'Not really, no. A bit unusual, I suppose. Longish. But it's just his name.'

'It isn't his name at all.'

'What!'

'Within a few seconds of hearing those two words, Jack, my mind turned to crosswords. You see, I may not be the greatest solver of puzzles in the world, but I have a go most days and I do know all the rules.'

'The rules?'

'Yes, the cryptic crossword rules. There are lots.'

He counted them off on the fingers of one hand.

'A question mark at the end of a clue often suggests a pun or a double meaning. When they include the word "unknown" it usually means an "x" or a "y". Words like "cardinal" or "point" might indicate the first letter of a compass point. For years you could be pretty sure that if a clue mentioned an "ancient city" the letters "ur" would crop up somewhere in the answer. Lots of little unwritten rules. You get used to spotting them. Now, when it comes to anagrams, I'll tell you something, Jack. It's very, very difficult for crossword compilers to successfully smuggle a longish anagram into a clue because it so often ends up looking a bit phoney, a bit too contrived. And when you have a go at the puzzle fairly frequently you learn to spot that awkward combination of letters and words. That's what happened when I heard the name "Daniel Tressingham". It was pure instinct. That, I said to myself, sounds all wrong. And after letting the whole thing roll around my head for a little while, I knew I was right.'

Jack's head was full of cotton wool. 'So you're saying he made that name up by rearranging the letters from some other word.'

'Or words.'

'Or words. So what was the original?'

'Try it for yourself.'

Doc took a pen from his inside pocket and reached up for a small square of white paper from the flowery notelet box on the dresser. He wrote for two or three seconds, then passed paper and pen across the table.

'There you are. Daniel Tressingham. Give you a clue. Three words, the middle one is "and".'

It was several minutes before Jack grunted in triumph and passed the pen back across the table.

'Nightmares and lies. Whose lies?'

'His own, of course. And his wife's.'

'Of course, that's what the whole thing was about, wasn't it? Nightmares and lies. But that's weird. Why didn't he tell us his real name?'

'The poor fellow was frightened,' said the Shadow Doctor. 'Terrified. He told me on the phone just now. He didn't know what was going to happen when he met me, who I was, what I might do, and he felt guilty and worried about people from his church hearing what had happened with the ill-named Naomi, so he just froze. Lost his nerve. His real name is Christopher Marsh. All the rest was true.

He apologised miserably and profusely for deceiving us. He's very happy now. I think he'll be OK.'

'Why is Naomi ill-named?'

'Naomi is an old Hebrew name. It means pleasantness, or pleasant and joyful. I can't truthfully say she's the former, and I'm quite sure she's not the latter at the moment. Perhaps,' he added softly, 'she will be both of those things one day.'

Jack nodded thoughtfully. 'And the rest of it? The trip to Tunbridge Wells to find a Halifax, and finding Kerry and Naomi in that place on the Pantiles when one of them should have been somewhere else? What about those trivial little details?'

'Ah, yes. Well, the bit about the Halifax is simple. I needed to get some money, and the local branch of my bank is closed on Saturdays. We strolled up there afterwards, didn't we? That was all very straightforward.'

'But that was all you said to Daniel – I mean to Christopher . . . whatever his name is. You didn't offer him any hope. Before we left here after breakfast, you just said you needed to go to the bank. That's all you said. I saw the expression on his face. He was so disappointed.'

Clasping his hands behind his head, the Shadow Doctor leaned back and frowned at the ceiling for a while. Finally, he brought his hands down onto his lap and nodded in agreement.

'You're quite right, Jack. By the way, he's still Daniel in my head as well. Let's go on calling him that for now. I do agree with you. I didn't offer Daniel any immediate hope. Perhaps it's something of a fault in me. A quirk. I really don't like promising gifts before I've actually got them to give. To put it another way, I was playing a hunch, and I was still just guessing.'

'But it was in this . . . this flow you keep talking about?'

'I thought it might be. And in the end, yes, I think so.'

'So what was it – the guess, I mean?'

'There were three, actually. First of all, everything I heard about Naomi suggested that she would have been dying to tell Kerry what happened between her and Daniel on the night of the party. I reckon she probably went and did exactly that soon after the event. A malicious confession. That was guess number one. The second guess was that Kerry would have been feeling so dreadful about hiding her past from Daniel and hurting him with her wild behaviour that she probably decided not to say anything to him about Naomi coming to spill the beans. She really didn't want him to feel bad about what he'd done. Now that is love. At the time this genuinely generous act of restraint would have spoiled Naomi's fun and annoyed her intensely, but later on it gave her an idea.

'At first she was only planning to blackmail Daniel, but when she learned from him that he had never spoken to his wife about what happened at the party, it struck her that she could do exactly the same to Kerry.'

'And this was guess number three?'

'Yes, I think the inspiration was hearing about Naomi's triumphant cry to her boyfriend or husband or whatever he is on the phone outside Daniel's office. Something about a "double whammy". Daniel assumed she was talking about the money from him on one hand, and the signed note about it being a repaid loan on the other. Well, that didn't seem much of a double whammy to me. Nothing double about it at all. What could she have meant? If my first two guesses were right, it was pretty simple. She thought she was going home with a thousand quid from each of them. When we got to the Pantiles and found Naomi sitting in Brown's with Kerry, I knew that my third guess had been spot on. Until that moment, though, I could have been completely wrong.'

Jack nodded. 'So Daniel and Kerry kept their money and Naomi went home with nothing. Gosh, she must have been spitting mad.'

'Yes, the journey home can't have been much fun. I wonder if her partner in crime met her at the station.'

Jack rested his chin on clenched hands as he thought through the events of the day. 'You took a big risk.'

'I did.'

'But you were right.'

The Shadow Doctor shrugged in a neutral sort of way, but said nothing.

'And Daniel and Kerry, they're OK, are they?'

'Judging by the way Daniel sounded on the phone just now, I'd say that they were very OK indeed. Probably playing Monopoly with real money and looking forward to bed. It doesn't get much better than that.'

'Good. So . . . do we thank God for a successful outcome?'

Jack would never have thought it possible for one spoken sentence to express openness and obfuscation at the same time. Doc managed it.

'Jack, you are free to do exactly as you choose. Be my guest.'

'I am your guest,' muttered Jack under his breath. 'But,' he added, opening his book and preparing to enjoy murder and mayhem in the City of Angels, 'I won't be for much longer if it goes on being all practice and no theory.'

11

The Lady Who Thought
She Might Explode

'I'm meeting a lady for coffee in Battle, Jack. She's afraid she might explode. Nice drive down through Hurst Green and Robertsbridge. About half an hour. One of my favourite cafés, The Wayfarer, not far from the abbey. Built in the fifteenth century for pilgrims and strangers and travellers and people like that. We can be whichever of those we choose. What do you think? Shall we be pilgrims? The place claims to have its own pet ghost. That might be fun.'

The Shadow Doctor flipped the case on his mobile shut and waggled it in his hand.

'Having foolishly promised that I'd meet her there, I've just checked to see if it's open. It is. On a day like this they'll probably get their wonderful fire lit. Fancy coming?'

A light breakfast had been cleared away. Jack, wrapped up warm in coat and scarf, had just returned from collecting an emptied wheelie bin from the lane at the end of the track so that it could be stowed away in the rickety shed next to the chicken run. Resisting an instinctive temptation to offer an opinion on the inadvisability of even considering the subject of ghosts, he glanced back through the open door and shivered. Outside, the sky above the forest was uncompromisingly sullen. Beyond the end of the drive, towards the south, a thick black curtain appeared to be rising inexorably. More rain on its way. The weather seemed intent on making a point. Now he was being invited to drive into the approaching storm to meet an exploding lady in some coffee house in Battle. Not for the first time, Jack wondered why Doc still seemed to find it necessary to cloak so many of his communications in cryptic obscurity. Was it worth asking? He decided to leave it until they were well on their way to Battle.

'Yes, of course. Why not? When do we need to leave?'

'Now would be perfect. Wake the silver monster. I'll get my coat and my new bright orange scarf. I'll lock up. See you outside in four minutes and thirty-seven seconds.'

Five minutes later Doc was about to climb into the passenger seat when he stopped and looked back towards the cottage.

'Sorry, Jack, I think I'll just pop back and get that piece of red silk I bought from the Oxfam in Tunbridge Wells last week. Won't be a moment. Keep the engine running.'

He was back in less than two minutes.

'Got it?'

The Shadow Doctor patted his inside jacket pocket with a gloved hand. 'Yep. Let's go.'

Jack toyed with the idea of asking why a large, florid sheet of material might be necessary to their expedition, but decided to leave it. Mentally, he added it to the growing list of questions that would have to wait. Just drive.

Jack quite enjoyed the in-car relationship that he was beginning to develop with the Shadow Doctor. Silences were less obtrusively tense, and sideways communication naturally allowed more scope for relaxed conversation. He was, however, determined to make no more enquiries about the reason for their trip until his companion brought it up. Nothing was said at all until they turned left onto the busy A21 and headed directly south. A light rain formed little cat's-paw patterns on the windscreen as they drove. The inside of the car felt warm and cosy, and, to Jack, pleasantly promising. Start with some comfortable trivia.

'Did you get enough breakfast, Doc? I'm afraid it was a bit skimpy this morning.'

'In the circumstances it was perfect, thank you, Jack. Exactly right.'

'What circumstances?'

'I only heard about today's trip while you were out with the bin. Thanks for doing that, by the way. You quite enjoy it, don't you? Dumping rubbish rather than constantly sorting through it is still a bit of a novelty for you, isn't it? As I let you know at a very early stage in your stay, getting the bins done is one of my least favourite jobs. It's funny, isn't it, how some not particularly complicated tasks can fill you with a sense of grinding tedium. I remember years ago we had a cat and a dog. They got fed at the same time every morning and evening. I got fed up at exactly the same times. When it was my turn to put the food down I did quite a bit of childish moaning and groaning. The cat's biscuits, the dog's biscuits, the cat's sachets, the dog's tin of meat, the dog's water. Fill the bowls up. Put the biscuit bags back under the sink. Make sure the half-used sachets and tins end up in the fridge. Let the dog out when she's finished. Let her back in. It seemed to go on for ever. Ridiculous, isn't it? Five minutes – that's all it took. Ridiculous.'

Jack drummed his fingers thoughtfully on the steering wheel. I will ask him one day, he thought. I'll get him to tell me about the other half of 'we'. Not now, though. Not yet. Dropping a hand, he flicked a switch to get some hot air on the windscreen. No more cat's paws. The rain was beating against the glass as if it wanted to come in and get dry. For a few minutes neither man spoke. Jack had to raise his voice to be heard above the rhythmic thump of the X-Trail's heavy-duty, elbow-like wipers.

'You said a small breakfast was perfect in the circumstances. What circumstances?'

'Oh yes, I'm so sorry, I do get a bit elliptic at times.'

'Do you?'

'It's very simple, really. All I meant was that there is one area of waste that has a more negative effect on day-to-day living than almost any other.'

'An area of waste? Like buying too much food and having to throw it away, you mean?'

'In a sense. I suppose that all waste is to do with throwing away something that other people might have used or enjoyed, but I'm talking about something very specific. I'm talking about waste of appetite.'

Jack turned the thought over in his mind, conscious suddenly that beneath the drumming of the wipers and the rattle of rain on the windscreen he could clearly hear the crackling buzz issuing from the X-Trail's tyres on the wet road. So many noises to separate and identify. So much to think about. How do you waste an appetite?

'Do you mean that you won't enjoy your coffee and scones or whatever else we have in this Battle place as much as if we'd had a big breakfast before leaving?'

'Well, yes, that was my immediate thought, but I think it goes much deeper than that. You must have already noticed that I have no problem with personal indulgence – on the contrary, I enjoy enjoying quite a lot of things. What I have learned, though . . .'

'Fine malt whisky.'

'Yes. What I have learned, though . . .'

'Whisky marmalade.'

'Yes, but . . .'

'Amazing wine.'

'Naturally.'

'Expensive posh overcoat.'

'Jack, shall we simply agree that the contents of the entire universe are available to me as and when I need them, and occasionally as treats. I am equally willing to embrace poverty. There is a strong precedent.'

Jack's fragile enjoyment at finding himself able to engage Doc in banter without losing his nerve was cut short by this last speech. He hadn't understood it, and he suspected that he wasn't intended to. He increased speed a little. The accelerator was the only thing available to kick. He allowed a small cloud of annoyance to dull his tone.

'What have you learned?'

'I have learned that a conscious decision to curb appetite in almost any area adds an essential edge to activities more worthy of expenditure, related or otherwise.'

'What sort of activities?'

The Shadow Doctor spread his gloved hands apart and tilted his head, indicating a broad range of options. 'Eating, drinking, sex, anything that needs close concentration, everything that involves people in need, totally unplanned time, decision-making – there are very few worthwhile things in life that don't benefit from the preservation of a keen appetite.'

The last item in Doc's list had sparked a thought in Jack's mind. It had also caused him to forget his sulk.

'Forty hungry days in which to make the three most important decisions in the history of the world?' he suggested tentatively.

Doc tapped the dashboard in front of him with the fingers of one hand, like a snooker player applauding his opponent's shot.

'Yes, thank you, forty days in which to choose and commit to the staple item of his diet.'

'Bread?'

Jack was vaguely hoping that he might be on a roll.

'No,' the Shadow Doctor smiled wryly as he turned his head. 'Obedience.'

Time passed. Jack glanced down at the sat-nav map on his phone.

'Eleven minutes to go. Passing Robertsbridge on our left. The weather's changed its mind. The sun's trying to come out. Are you going to tell me about . . .'

The Shadow Doctor leaned forward to peer through the windscreen as he interrupted. 'Robertsbridge! Malcolm and Kitty used to live just up the road from the village. Hilaire Belloc started his famous fictitious walk of four men to the beautiful valley of the Arun from the George Inn at the top of the High Street. And there is also . . .'

'Who were Malcolm and Kitty? Who is Hilaire Belloc? Who were the four men?'

'The Muggeridges. He was an author and broadcaster. She spent a lot of time waiting for him to come home. He wrote like an angel. Became a Christian late in life. I knew him a little then. Belloc was another writer. The four men were different aspects of his own personality, as far as I've been able to understand what he was getting at. He produced poetry, history, fiction, children's rhymes, all sorts of stuff. A Catholic. Friend of G.K. Chesterton. Died in the 1950s. Very keen on the truth. I was just about to say that there's also a very fine Indian restaurant called New Spice in Robertsbridge.'

'Not that we shall be wasting our precious appetites in that establishment on this occasion,' muttered Jack wryly to himself.

Try something completely different.

'Why is your new orange scarf so important to you?'

Doc smiled and touched the lurid material with his fingers before replying. 'I'm not a very bright orange person, Jack. I need to change a little in that respect. I think you could help me with that.'

Jack shot a glance at the other man. 'I'm not sure I want to know what that means.'

The Shadow Doctor guffawed loudly. 'I'm not sure I do either, but I promise you it's not an insult. Somebody very wise tried to brighten me up for years, but I never co-operated. I hate my scarf. I love it as well. I hope she can see me now.'

He turned his face away. Jack said nothing. There was nothing to say. He took another quick look at his phone. 'Where do we go when we get into Battle? We'll be there in a minute.'

'Right. There's a roundabout at the top of the town. When we get there you'll be able to see the abbey at the bottom of the High Street. Halfway down there's a turning on the left. Mount Street, I think it is. The car park's along that road on the right. There's a little winding path from there through to the shops.'

'Are you going to tell me anything about this exploding lady?'

A watery sun was transfiguring the rain-drenched road into a glittering ribbon of light as the Shadow Doctor sighed in defeat and began to answer Jack's question.

'Jack, I know only three things for sure about this lady.'

He tapped one forefinger heavily against the other as he went through his list.

'First, her Christian name is Samantha. Second, she fears that she might explode – I have no idea what that means, by the way. If you want to know why we are taking so much time and trouble to meet and listen to this particular individual, the answer is tied up with the third thing that I know for sure. Samantha is, without doubt, the most important person in the world. We must keep remembering that when we meet her.'

The pronoun at the front end of Doc's last sentence brought a glow to Jack's heart. But how fickle was he? Sulking and glowing within the same half-hour journey, for goodness' sake. Bin the sulk. Hold the glow.

Jack found a good space for the bulky X-Trail at the bottom end of the car park, less than twenty yards from the narrow alley that would take them through to the High Street. A smart lady with sculpted ash-blonde hair and a friendly smile was about to get back into the next-but-one car in the row, a gleaming BMW saloon. Leaning across the bonnet of the intervening vehicle, she offered her Pay and Display ticket to them.

'There's more than an hour left on it,' she announced with a sort of muted cheeriness. 'I got away from the doctor's really quickly for once. I've got an extra hour to fill. You might as well use it.'

For some time Jack had been thinking differently about the sentences that automatically formed themselves in his head on occasions like this. Previously he might have claimed and almost believed that they were spoken by the Holy Spirit. Now he was confused. That prompting voice was sounding more and more like an officious special constable at the end of an uneventful shift. As it was, any temptation to refuse the ticket on the grounds that acceptance would be tantamount to theft was eclipsed by Doc's immediate, smiling acceptance of the nice lady's offer.

'Thank you so much,' he said warmly, 'I'm glad you got away early. How will you use your unexpected extra hour? Something really nice, I hope.'

She stared at him for a moment, the smile fading from her face as she passed the strap of a lemon yellow handbag from side to side through beautifully manicured fingers.

'Nothing's very nice at the moment. An empty hour is quite hard. My husband died two and a half . . . nearly three months ago. I've not been very good at enjoying things since then, I'm afraid. I do try, but I don't think I ever realised just how long an hour could be – sixty minutes dragging me down like a necklace of lead weights.'

She collected herself a little.

'I'm so sorry – I've been wanting to say that to someone for quite a while. I really don't know why it had to be you.'

'It doesn't matter,' said Doc quietly, 'I'm glad you did. Just before you go and deal with your hellish hour, would you let me say one thing to you?'

She nodded, rather like a small child lost on a crowded pavement.

Moving to her side, the Shadow Doctor began to speak, his voice too low for Jack to hear what was being said. He checked the time on his phone. This Samantha person was waiting for them – probably feeling quite nervous – and they were already a couple of minutes late. Why was Doc allowing himself to be distracted by someone who had been drawn in by his extraordinary capacity for making random folk feel safe and valued? Surely it was reasonable to erect appropriate fences where they were necessary and helpful.

These thoughts, pompous even to Jack's own inner ear, were interrupted by a peal of laughter from the lady with the blue bag. After a further brief verbal exchange, she lightly embraced the figure standing before her and turned away, stopping to give a quick, slightly embarrassed wave before getting into her car. Moments later she backed the BMW out, turned it to face in the direction of the exit, and was gone.

'What did you say to make her laugh like that?'

'I'll tell you on the way home.'

'We're going to be late. Was she the most important person in the world as well?'

The Shadow Doctor held his gaze. 'Yes, she was and is. Lock the car. Let's go.'

12

The Wayfarer

Jack fell in love with The Wayfarer at first sight. Beneath a red-tiled roof the ancient timber-framed Tudor building featured what he vaguely identified as mullioned windows of various shapes and sizes, some tiny, some long and thin, others puzzlingly wide. A few were shaped like perfect honeycombs.

The approach was along a brick path leading down some age-worn steps to an old oak door with long, creaking iron hinges and a heavy ring handle. A second door, so low that both men needed to duck their heads, gave entrance to the main chamber, a room whose vast size came as a shock to Jack after negotiating the claustrophobic access.

The Shadow Doctor smiled at the expression on his companion's face. 'Bit of a Tardis, Jack?'

The young man shook his head in wonder. 'Amazing. It's quite fantastic. So big. So high.'

The lofty ceiling was supported by centuries-old timbers and one massive post stretching from the floor to the centre of the roof. In one corner a crazily uneven staircase disappeared into the mysterious darkness of a mezzanine floor, perhaps a gallery for musicians in the distant past. Odd-shaped wooden tables stood haphazardly around the room, accompanied by mainly rush-seat chairs. A few wooden chairs equipped with shelves for hymn books were dotted about, presumably refugees from some church that was either closing or refurbishing. Against a long rear window stood a bench distorted by use over the ages to such an extent that the resultant shape would probably have greatly puzzled its maker.

The walls were a mixture of exposed brickwork and occasional patches of damaged plaster, the floors wooden and worn down by hundreds of human feet through the ages. Iron candle chandeliers hung from the high ceiling, but did not seem to be in use. Perhaps, thought Jack, modern customers were likely to be less than tolerant of candle wax dripping onto them from a great height. In this age discreet spotlights gave the only visible illumination in an otherwise dark interior. The most heart-and-body-warming feature of the room was the fireplace, an authentic-looking inglenook stacked with piles of logs on either side. A large open wood stove threw out immense heat, giving off a fiery red glow tinged with orange flame. The chimney itself towered to the full height of the room.

This is a wonderful environment, thought Jack, a magic castle in the real world. A place where something might happen.

There was only one other customer in the restaurant, a dark-haired woman sitting on her own with her back to the door at one of the tables nearest to the fire. She looked up nervously as the two men appeared.

Doc extended a hand. 'You must be Samantha.'

'Sam. It's Sam usually. You must be . . .'

'Doc. Call me Doc. This is my friend Jack. He urgently needs coffee. Me too. Can I get one for you?'

She indicated the empty cup in front of her on the table, her eyes darting from one to the other as she spoke. 'You can get me another one. Or I think they do a cafetière. We could get one for all of us. The waitress will come over in a minute.' She giggled. 'I shouldn't call her that. She's far too posh and in charge to be a waitress – even if she is one. Probably the owner. Friendly, though.'

Jack pulled out a chair and sat down. He liked Sam straightaway. It was the way she looked. It made him feel more confident. A sweet face, full of sorrow and playfulness. Her hair was cut in a neat bob, framing a round, homely face, illuminated by a pair of large blue eyes and a mouth that seemed to twitch as though in anticipation of amusement. Probably in her late forties or early fifties. Almost certainly wrong about that. He had no faith at all in his ability to assess a woman's age. She certainly didn't look like someone who was likely to explode.

Doc reached for a menu. 'Shall we have something to eat as well, Sam? I'd like something. Teacake, cheese scone, piece of cake? All three? Our treat.'

Sam's posh waitress appeared. Tall, vigorous and crystalline in speech, she took their order with smiling efficiency and placed a laminated sheet of A4 paper in the middle of the table before turning away towards the kitchen.

'Bit of the history,' she announced over her shoulder. 'The ghost is a fact. I've seen her.'

'Her?'

The waitress stopped and turned to face Sam. 'Yes, Tudor lady in a long grey dress with one of those big concertina ruffs. Not very original really, is it? Perhaps the stuff in the ghost costume store is more off-the-peg than bespoke. Even the spook world is doing it on the cheap. I'll be right back with your order.'

Sam, eyes wide with mock solemnity, whispered, 'Do you think she's serious?'

'Quite probably,' replied Doc lightly. 'Making a place like this pay its way is difficult enough as it is. I think I'd be very serious about keeping an in-house ghost going for as long as possible, wouldn't you? Especially during the months when our closest allies invade Battle and demand cream teas and a bit of a thrill.'

Jack opened his mouth and shut it again. Sam chuckled appreciatively.

Minutes later a large cafetière arrived, closely followed by what Doc described as three discus-sized teacakes, each one sliced through and soaked with butter.

'Enjoy!'

With a flourish and a neat little bow, the modern Amazon took her leave. The cafetière plunger was plunged after the usual correct interval, and teacakes were distributed. After one sip of his coffee the Shadow Doctor seemed to sink a couple of inches and become one with his chair, a picture of utter contentment.

'Ah, Sam! Thank you so much for providing us with a reason to come here this morning. I love interesting surroundings, I love good coffee, I love giant teacakes drenched in butter, and I love good company. To paraphrase what my Jewish brothers and sisters sing during their Passover meal – if you had only made it possible to have these things on this morning, *Dayenu!*'

'"It would have been enough for us",' quoted Sam. 'That's what that word means, isn't it? And – is that really true?'

'It's certainly true for us. It might not be enough for you. Let me tell you one thing that is certainly true. I know we've only just met, but I really like you. I like your broken, laughing, frightened, hopeful heart.'

No one speaks like that, thought Jack – no one I've ever known. Not minutes into a relationship.

'Most of all,' continued Doc, 'I like your courage in coming here.'

He could have been talking about teacakes. The blue eyes silvered with tears. Doc didn't seem to notice. He waved a hand in the younger man's direction.

'Jack, we've known Sam for about . . . fifteen minutes? That's about one hundredth of a butterfly's life. Long time. So . . .'

Sam smiled through her tears. 'One ninety-sixth, to be precise.'

'Good heavens! Well, yes, that is true, unless of course the butterfly in question hasn't actually lived for exactly one day. In which case it could be less or more, or . . . anyway, what I was going to ask you, Jack, is this. Do *you* like Sam?'

Jack froze. His contribution to the conversation so far had been less than distinguished. Pretty well non-existent, in fact. Words like 'irresponsible' and 'thoughtless' and 'ill-judged' flew around the inside of his head, only to flutter into extinction as he realised that he knew, as surely as it was possible to know anything, that the Shadow Doctor would never have asked him the question if there had been any doubt about his answer.

Tell the truth.

The truth. Jack's habit had been to corral most of his feelings in readiness for some kind of safe translation. An exhausting business. Mostly it never got done. Perhaps this would be easier. Perhaps. Sam's eyes, regarding him over the top of her coffee mug, expressed nothing but sympathy. He cleared his throat.

'I know it sounds silly, Sam, but I think I liked you as soon as I saw you. You made me feel – I don't know – more sure of myself. You've got such a friendly face. I was feeling a bit nervous about meeting you. I mean, all we really knew about you was that you were frightened of . . . well . . .'

'Frightened that I might explode? I'm sorry, you must have thought I was off my head. But when I called the number I'd been given, the very nice lady who answered wanted to know what was troubling me, and I said I was very afraid. Then she asked me to tell her exactly what that meant, and the honest answer was . . . well, I was terrified that I would explode. That was that. No more questions. No more discussion. She told me someone would call me, and you did. And here I am. By the way, I'm very glad that you both like me, but I'm really not that keen on either of you.'

Jack felt his body jerk half an inch backwards with the shock, but the Shadow Doctor just smiled and nodded.

'Jack, I rather fancy that was a little jest. I think Sam has decided that she might have to trust us.'

He raised his eyebrows in a question.

Sam nodded ruefully. 'Sorry, I do say really silly things sometimes. Sorry, Jack, I loved what you said. I honestly did. I suppose I was just a bit embarrassed.'

'Tell us what it's all about, Sam. Hold on – wait while I order some more coffee. We're bound to need it.'

*　　*　　*

A fresh cafetière had arrived. Sam glanced quickly over both shoulders in turn at the room behind her as Jack carefully topped up their mugs.

'I don't know if there really are any ghosts in this place, but to be honest they wouldn't scare me very much. I'm not frightened of things like that. On the contrary, they might be quite fun. A bit of a distraction from . . . from what I'm really afraid of.'

'Do you believe in God, Sam?'

If it had been possible, Jack would have taken the question back as soon as it came out. A verse from the Bible about perfect love casting out fear had come into his mind. Perhaps it was true. But it was equally true that, even if the love of God was perfect, it had never cast out all the fear from his mind. Oh well, it was said now. He glanced at Doc. Just a little whimsical twist of the lips. He didn't seem worried.

'The answer to your question, Jack, is that I am a Christian in the sense that William Topaz McGonagall was a poet. The difference between us is that he wouldn't even have understood the question. Actually, that's a bit unfair on God. I think I've always suspected deep in my heart that God might have got something wonderful all stored up for me, despite my sad, thin little shot at being a Christian, whatever that means. My problem is that, in a way, I hope he hasn't.'

A strange, sad silence fell. Doc broke it very gently.

'Who are your ghosts, Sam?'

Sam tilted her head back as though to prevent a sudden overflow. When she spoke, her voice was quiet and unemotional, but her eyes were bleak, staring into a familiar darkness.

'The ones I lost. All the ones I lost who might have taught me what it means to be loved. My father died when I was little, my mother soon after, then my brother. Later, my baby daughter and my husband, within months of each other. I know it must sound a bit melodramatic, but there's a sadness inside me so profound that the blinking thing seems to have soaked every cell in my body. Over the years I've struggled with a fantasy in which all those lost ones got on a train and went off to some other station without telling me where they were going. They just left me behind and I'm alone.'

She checked for half a second.

'That's not actually true, of course. I'm not alone, but I don't believe I shall ever catch them up again, those ghosts of mine.

'They do visit every now and then. I come downstairs in the morning and think I hear a tiny noise in the kitchen. My heart seems to stop. My mother's in there. She's holding little Maisie in her arms. I'll go in there and Mum will smile and Maisie will chuckle, and the kitchen will fill with light and the love will pour and pour and pour into me and around me and over me until all the sadness is washed away and everything will be . . . perfect. Sometimes, when I'm walking along the High Street near where I live, I see a car go past driven by a man who looks a bit like the photo of my dad that I've got at home. I hurry up a bit in case it really is him and he's come back to find me. He might not recognise me now that I'm much older. Imagine if I missed him. He would be so sad.'

Sensing the atmosphere she had created, Sam smiled and flapped a hand reassuringly.

'Don't worry, I've still got my marbles. I know my mum's never going to turn up in my kitchen. My dad's dead. Little Sam inside me makes up stories. It's just imagination. A sort of wish generator that fires itself up from time to time.'

Doc nodded thoughtfully.

'Someone has loved you, Sam. I can see it in you. I'm glad. But who is it? Who is the special person in your life?'

Sam hesitated for a moment.

'Chris is the special person in my life. We became friends a long time ago and eventually just sort of . . . slipped into loving each other. We're quite different, but we help each other to cope. A lot more than that. I don't know what I'd do without Chris.'

The Shadow Doctor gave her a quizzical look. 'I'm sure he feels the same.'

A beat.

'She. She feels the same. Chris is a lady. We're a . . . a same-sex couple.'

Sam flicked a glance from one man to the other, reminding Jack of a small, apprehensive animal peeping out of its burrow at a potential predator.

Ask her how they met.

'How did you and Chris meet, Sam?'

The creature popped, wide-eyed, into the open, apparently shocked out of its nervousness by Jack's question. Sam smiled apologetically.

'I'm sorry if I looked shocked, Jack. It was your question. I suppose I've got a bit wary. Some of the people I've told about Chris and me . . . well, something changes in their eyes. They either start being terribly kind to me, or they shift uneasily and look as if they want to make something very clear. It was so unusual – so nice – to hear someone ask such a gloriously normal question.'

Jack sat very still and tried not to look too kind. 'Good. So, how did you meet?'

'Oh, it was on a bus. Chris was sitting next to me, and I was by the window lost in a little fantasy about Maisie being next to me. I was talking to her inside my head, but I'm afraid I got a bit carried away. A few words slipped out by accident. I said, really loudly, "Ooh, look at the pretty moocows!" Chris agreed with me that they were really lovely moocows, and we laughed like drains for the rest of the trip. It all started there. The way it worked out was a . . . a wonderful surprise, for both of us.'

Nobody spoke for a few seconds. Doc reached across to pour the last dribble of coffee into Sam's mug.

'Why are you frightened of exploding?'

Sam swallowed the dribble, set her mug down, blinked, and took a deep breath.

'It's about heaven. They don't have tears in heaven, do they? That's what the Bible says. I'm made of tears. That's me! Why would all those smiling people want me around making them feel miserable? And it's all about the fact that ultimate love, I mean the sort of love that might actually be able to overwhelm and transform – transfigure – the essential sorrowful me, is just too frightening to contemplate. How would I survive it? I don't think I would. I think I would explode. I really do. Bits of my fragile, undernourished little psyche littering the streets of gold. An extra job for some garbage-clearing novice angel.'

She shook her head in sorrowful resignation.

'So, there's one obvious conclusion, isn't there? No heaven for me. Although I always say I believe everyone else will get there. Except, of course, those who feel the same as me – if they exist. Maybe I don't really believe that. In fact, in the middle of the night and when even the ghosts don't turn up, I'm not certain there is a heaven at all. And if any or all of the things I've just said are true – that the options boil down to oblivion, exclusion or explosion – what's left? Who's in charge of the hope bank? Where can I get some?'

She stared at her clasped hands for a few seconds before continuing with increased passion.

'Believe me, Jack, Doc, I want it all, I honestly do. I want that *Railway Children* moment where I meet the heavenly Father who loves me, and it's all right, and I don't explode, and I don't have to be made of misery any more. I so want . . . all that.'

Big round tears rolled down Sam's cheeks as she began to sob silently. Jack watched in dismay. What was the best thing to do?

'Here,' said the Shadow Doctor. 'Use this.'

Reaching into his jacket pocket, he removed the folded sheet of red silk that he had placed there before leaving the house, shook it loose and, rising from his seat, floated it across the table. It was ridiculously large, settling like a crimson cloud over Sam's head and shoulders. She pulled the clinging silk from her face with both hands and looked at it in amazement.

'What's this?'

'It's my joke handkerchief,' replied Doc calmly. 'I keep it for, you know, situations like this.'

Sam threw her head back and burst into laughter.

121

'That is so *silly*! That is so ridiculously silly.'

Dabbing her eyes with a paper napkin, she screwed the shiny material into an unwieldy ball and threw it back across the table.

'You are a very silly man. You do know that, don't you? I love it. I love silly. Much better than most comfort and counselling. Laughter is my favourite shortcut; that and perfectly chilled Chardonnay. By the way, you'll be pleased to note that I did not blow my nose on your beautiful joke handkerchief. Snot and silk. That would have been disgusting.'

Doc was happily and carefully refolding his scarlet extravaganza.

'It would. Thank you for your restraint.'

'Sam, I want all those things that you talked about just now,' said Jack quietly, 'and I have to confess that I'm a bit worried myself about whether I'm going to be allowed to have them in the end. Can I ask you something?'

'Of course. If it's about my personal gallery of erotica, I may have to lie, but you're very welcome to ask.'

An image of his gran smiling broadly at her nephew's discomfiture entered Jack's mind for a split second. Push on.

'Why do you bother? You seem to have a passionate desire – a sort of deep longing – for someone to keep the promises that have never given you what you want, and, if you're right about the exploding thing, probably never will. You even said that there are times when you don't believe in heaven at all. Why does it go on being so important?'

As he finished speaking, Jack became aware that Doc was regarding him with an expression of interested appraisal. It was, after all, a very Shadow-Doctorish question.

'Well, first of all, I'm quite sure I'm not alone in doubting all sorts of things. That's not unusual. No, I suppose the real answer to your question, however silly it might sound, is that, although I might go off bang in the end, the only little ledge of firm ground that I can manage to find is next to Puddleglum, the marsh-wiggle who makes that wonderful speech to the Queen of Underland in *The Silver Chair* after hurting his foot by stamping out her fire. He's my hero.'

Jack smiled and nodded as his mind flew to the scene she had described. *The Silver Chair* was a favourite. He knew and loved Lewis's Narnia books. The Shadow Doctor obviously knew them even better. He quoted softly.

'"Suppose we have only dreamed, or made up, all those things – trees and grass and sun and moon and stars and Aslan himself. Suppose we have. Then all I can say is that, in that case, the made-up things seem a good deal more important than the real ones. Suppose this black pit of a kingdom of yours is the only world. Well, it strikes me as a pretty poor one. And that's a funny thing, when you come to think of it. We're just babies making up a game, if you're right. But four babies playing a game can make a play-world which licks your real world hollow. That's why I'm going to stand by the play world. I'm on Aslan's side even if there isn't any Aslan to lead it. I'm going to live as like a Narnian as I can even if there isn't any Narnia. So, thanking you kindly for our supper, if these two gentlemen and the young lady are ready, we're leaving your court at once and setting out in the dark to spend our lives looking for

Overland. Not that our lives will be very long, I should think; but that's a small loss if the world's as dull a place as you say."

'That book lives by my side of the bed. I read Puddleglum's speech every time I start to sink under the weight of the worst loss in my life. I believe in Overland. I've walked in it quite often over the last few years, but when that aching gap in my existence becomes a great big ugly chasm of sorrow and uncertainty, I stand with the marsh-wiggle as well.'

He paused for a moment, seemingly unsure whether to add to what he had said.

'I sometimes think that when I stand with him I'm actually standing with someone else altogether.'

Sam's eyes were bright with tears once more. She spoke in a whisper. 'What do you mean?'

'Once, I saw or imagined or dreamed that Jesus had come to find me in the dark. He brought his own light with him. First of all he showed me his wounds, feet, hands and side. And then . . .'

For the first time since their initial encounter, Jack heard a catch in Doc's voice as he continued.

'And then, he asked me to show him my wounds. I pointed to my heart. There was one of those never-going-to-end moments, then he invited me to take his arm, and we set off together through the darkness to find a way back to Overland.'

Doc broke the spell he had created by reverting to his more accustomed tone of smiling self-deprecation.

'I know we have a tendency to dream or imagine the things we want, but whether it was a product of inspiration or indigestion doesn't really matter. That little encounter meant a lot to me.' He paused. 'I've not mentioned it to a living soul until now.'

Sam's head was tilted in sympathy. She reached across to squeeze the Shadow Doctor's hand.

'I'm so sorry about your loss. And the wound in your heart. I really am.'

Jack felt a momentary spasm of jealousy and isolation. Was this developing loop elastic enough to include him? How silly. He did his best to dismiss the thought. Today was about Sam. Wasn't it?

'Can I get you anything else, guys?'

There was a smile in the Amazon's voice as she loomed stylishly, but the meaning was clear. Time to go.

'No thanks,' said Doc cheerily. 'Just the bill, please.'

'I'll be straight back.'

Sam picked up a cloth bag from the chair next to her own. She suddenly looked a little uncertain.

'I'm not sure what we do now. I mean – did you want to pray for me or something?'

'No need,' said Doc, passing a folded slip of paper across the table. 'Read this later.'

'Oh. Right. OK. Thanks.'

Looking a little bemused, she dropped it into a side pocket and lifted a purse from her bag. 'Are you going to let me pay?'

'No. We might let you pay something next time.'

'Next time? Is there going to be a next time?'

The Shadow Doctor looked a little sheepish. 'I've really enjoyed this, Sam. Forgive me, it's a bit self-indulgent, but whether or not we can be of any use to you, I'd love it if we could get together again. You'd enjoy that, wouldn't you, Jack?'

'I really would,' replied Jack, pleased and relieved that it was true. 'We could go out to dinner. Bring Chris.'

Sam brightened like a little girl who has been promised a treat. Her blue eyes shone. 'She would love that. So would I – if you really mean it.'

'We mean it,' said the Shadow Doctor. 'I'll give you a ring. Maybe we should call ourselves the Marsh-Wiggle Club. We could be founder members.'

'Shall we all wear the hats?'

'It would be wicked not to. That can be your job. Here comes the bill. I'll see you both outside.'

Five minutes later, standing in front of the abbey gates, they were about to part when Sam asked to be allowed two more questions.

'Doc, what's it like in Overland?'

The Shadow Doctor answered very seriously. 'I suspect you've been there more often than you dare to believe, Sam, but I will say how it seems to me. Let me see. It's confusing, exciting, tough, filled with surprises, frightening, wonderful, demoralising and inspiring. Come to think of it, I might as well end the list there. There aren't many things that it isn't. I'll tell you one thing, though. It appears to exist, and it may interest you to hear that, as far as I know, there is no record of anyone exploding there – not yet, anyway.'

'Thank you.'

'Your second question?'

'Oh yes.' She returned his steady gaze. 'It's this. Just before I go. A small thing. You and Jack. You're top chaps.

I've loved our time together. Really looking forward to meeting up again and introducing you to Chris. But my question is – who are you?'

'I might tell you next time,' said Doc, when the laughter had subsided.

13

Loose Ends

'Did you enjoy going into Battle today, Jack?'

Five minutes of the return journey had passed. Above, the brittle sun still shone from a sky as blue as a hedge-sparrow's egg, but ahead of them in the north a suspension of impossibly dense white cloud hung like a heavy drift of snow in the air.

As he drove, Jack was doing his best to process feelings and thoughts about their encounter with Sam, replaying snatches of conversation, moments that had seemed significant, worrying or illuminating. Doc had said something about 'my side of the bed'. He certainly had no intention of bringing that up.

Apart from anything else, he found himself buzzing with restrained excitement over a germ of a realisation that the narrow gateway of simple truth seemed to be offering him access to a route that might ultimately be more liberating and straightforward than the equally narrow but far less productive road that he had battled to negotiate until very recently. Could it be, he thought, smiling a little at his own question, that the Bible really was true after all?

Doc's question was the first time either of the two men had spoken. Jack decided to ignore the deliberate ambiguity for now.

'Yes I did, very, very much. It was quite exciting. Being in that amazing place. Meeting Sam and finding she was so attractive – in the best sense, I mean.'

'Not in the dreaded worst sense, then?' The Shadow Doctor's tone was strictly neutral.

Jack freed a hand from the wheel and rapped his companion's arm lightly. 'You know exactly what I mean. She was so lovely. She made me feel good. Sad as well. The bit about her mum and her baby in the kitchen.' He shook his head. 'Just thinking about it now brings tears to my eyes. I think she was made for laughing. It seems such a shame.'

He cleared his throat before continuing. 'I did feel a little bit jealous when you talked about your . . . you know, your experience, and she was suddenly comforting you instead of the other way round. I knew it was silly straightaway, though. I've always felt cold and lost when I think I'm being pushed outside. Ridiculous, isn't it?'

'You were wonderful today, Jack. Did you see how Sam reacted when you asked how she and Chris met? Where did that come from?'

'I'm not quite sure,' replied Jack, so overcome by being described as wonderful that he found it difficult to speak. 'In a way, that wasn't quite me. It just seemed . . . I don't know how to put it. It just seemed the right thing to say. Do you know what I mean?'

Doc nodded thoughtfully. 'Mm, yes, I believe I do.'

Jack pushed himself back in the driving seat, straightening his arms to retain a grip on the wheel.

'I've got a few questions for you, if that's all right.'

The Shadow Doctor performed a positive twirling movement with the forefinger of one raised hand. 'Not a problem, as long as you don't expect me to answer them straightforwardly. I'm not used to this.'

'You don't mind, though?'

Doc sighed. 'Ask your questions, Jack.'

'A small one first. Why do you always lock your door so carefully when you live in the middle of a wood miles from anywhere and you're so laid back about everything else?'

Doc screwed his face up and made tutting noises. 'Hm, you're really making me work. I lock my door because I've learned at considerable cost that you can't take anything for granted. Securing my little house may not make much sense, but it is a mark of trust.'

That makes even less sense, thought Jack. Never mind. Press on.

'OK. Next question. The red silk. What you called your joke handkerchief. When you went back to get it this morning, did you have any idea at all that you might be using it in the way you did?'

'No.'

'Is it really what you call your joke handkerchief?'

Doc shrugged. 'Well, it is now. It wasn't. I made that up on the spot.'

'Why did you take it at all?'

'No idea. Just thought it might come in useful.'

'The flow?'

Doc shrugged again. 'Flowish.'

Jack drove in silence for a minute or two, his brow furrowed in thought. When he spoke again it was with troubled passion, like a buried frustration brought to the surface.

'You see, it's like the time you first met my gran. What made you go down and sit in that shelter? Did you know you were going to meet someone there?'

'No. I like storms. I like all the wild and the wet and the chaos of a thumping good storm. And I absolutely love being under cover looking out at the weather. Better than going to the films. I was very happy sitting there, taking in the sounds and the sights and trying to think of a rhyme for crocuses.'

Jack decided to ignore the red herring for once. 'OK, so it was all random, was it? You just happened to be there, and Gran just happened to turn up at the same time, and then you just happened to go back to the flat and save her life. That was all chance and random, was it?'

Doc's face was filled with the confusion and discomfort of someone who has been asked entirely the wrong question and is finding the weight of adjustment difficult to handle. 'Jack, the nearest I can get to it is that it was a random step in a non-random context. Does that make any sense?'

'No. What's a non-random context? Are we talking about the blessed flow again? Being in the flow? Were you in the flow?'

The Shadow Doctor shook his head wearily. 'Oh dear, sometimes our own metaphors come back to haunt us, don't they? I'm getting very bored with the flow. I suppose I mean that I was very confident about being in Eastbourne. That was the context. As for what might happen there – no idea. Not a clue.'

'How did you know you should be in Eastbourne?'

'All I can tell you is that I was as filled up with that knowledge as you and I are sometimes filled up with breakfast.

My friend George suggested it. That was that. I knew straightaway that it was right.'

'And George is . . . ?'

'My friend. George is my friend.'

Jack fell silent. He never had been good at disobeying NO ENTRY signs. He did have something else to say, though. The words were difficult to get out.

'Doc, I never thanked you for . . . I wanted to thank you for . . . you know . . . helping Alice, my gran, to get through the time when she decided to end her own life. I was ever so upset when I first read about her deciding to do that. It . . . it burned me inside to think that she felt such awful despair and didn't want to tell me or let me help her. We were so close. It hurt.'

'Of course.'

'But I am grateful. I really loved her.'

'I know you did. It's nice that you're grateful, Jack, but all I really did was play Scrabble with her.'

'Well, it wasn't, but . . . can I ask you something about that?'

The Shadow Doctor sighed once more and managed a smile. 'Go ahead.'

'Just before you suggested that to Gran – the Scrabble game, I mean – what was in your mind? The person sitting in front of you had just told you she was planning to end her life. What were your thoughts?'

'I hope it won't disappoint you to learn that I didn't really have any. I suppose it's a sort of policy of mine to throw conversations off balance in difficult situations. That's why I agreed with Alice that suicide probably was the logical solution to her problem. Other than that, though, I don't think there was an idea in my head. However, I did know,' he added quite firmly, 'that I would do something. And that something turned out to be ordinary old Scrabble.'

He reflected for a moment. 'Also, I'm sure you won't misunderstand me, Jack, when I say that, in the most refined and restrained sense, there was a whiff of flirtatiousness about that first encounter, and the occasional meetings we had subsequently were most enjoyable for both of us. Our friendship was a new thing in Alice's life. Perhaps it moved her blood around a little faster.'

Jack was smiling.

'You don't have to worry about calling Gran a flirt. She made me blush like a schoolboy sometimes. I love the thought of her looking forward to seeing you. I bet she put on a bit of a show.'

Doc chuckled reminiscently. 'You're right. She did make a bit of an effort. Perm, pearls and a posh frock, that's what she always promised. She was a wonderful lady. Never did beat me at Scrabble, though. If I had deliberately let her win she would never have spoken to me again. You knew your grandma better than I did.'

Memories darted around their heads like fireflies for a minute or two. Jack was frowning again.

'There's something I still can't get my head round. You and her meeting in the storm, going back to the flat, the Scrabble, your visits after that, everything that happened – was that God, or coincidence, or both, or neither, or what?'

The Shadow Doctor collected his thoughts.

'It was a stew, a very tasty, nourishing stew.'

'Yes, but . . .'

'Tell you what, later today at home, or tomorrow morning if we run out of time, just say the word "onion" to me and I'll try very hard to give you a proper answer to your question.'

'Onion.'

'Yes, just say that word so I don't forget.'

'Why can't you tell me now?'

'There has to be an onion present,' said Doc solemnly.

Jack breathed in heavily through his nose. Wonderful as he might be, he would have liked to maintain a dignified silence for the rest of the journey, but he still had three questions to ask, and it was hard to see how onions could possibly feature in the answers to any of them.

'You gave Sam a slip of paper when she asked if we were going to pray for her. What was written on that?'

'Ah, now that's much easier to answer. I usually keep a couple of those little slips in one of my pockets. It's a verse from the book of Malachi – or Malarky, as I heard someone mistakenly and gloriously call it once. Malachi is one long rant by God about people dumping their rubbish livestock on the altar instead of the best they had. False fire was another thing he hated. Still does, and there's a lot of it about.'

'So what happened?'

'Eventually, folk got together to talk about the problem, and in one translation Malachi 3:16 says that God "received their conversation as prayer". Takes some of the pressure off, don't you think? From the moment we met Sam to the moment we parted, that's what was happening. Next time might be different. We'll see.'

'That brings me to my next question. Do you think Sam was helped by meeting us today? I mean, I think she enjoyed it, but it's not going to make much difference to all that deep-down unhappiness, is it? By the way, I thought it was really good how you let her feel that she was doing you a favour by arranging to meet again.'

The Shadow Doctor became very still. The temperature in the car changed noticeably.

'Jack, I did no such thing. I didn't let her feel anything. I meant every word I said. We both took to Sam, and I have an idea we're going to get on very well with Chris as well. I wanted Sam to know that we weren't organising some sort of ghastly second phase of treatment. As to whether she was helped by our meeting – I don't really know, but it did me quite a lot of good. I'll tell you what we do. We make real friends. We go with it. We keep our eyes and ears open. We don't assume anything. We wait to see what happens. We are only charged with loving people. The rest is not our responsibility.'

Jack came close to crying, but the chilled voice seemed to have frozen his blood and his tears. So tangled were his thoughts and feelings that he was unable to embark on the reasonable task of finding out how his words could have provoked such a response. He felt small and silly. An amateur being told off by a professional. An apology could surely not make things worse.

'I'm sorry. I'm very sorry. I didn't understand.'

They drove on in silence until a large letter 'P' announced a layby half a mile up the road.

'There's a parking place coming up,' said Doc in a very different tone of voice. 'Pull in there, would you? Let's stop for a moment.'

Nothing more was said until the car came to a standstill on a small, uneven crescent of tarmac fringed with silver birches. Jack switched the engine off. Silence apart from a faint ticking somewhere under the bonnet. There were no other vehicles in the layby. Resting his crossed hands on top of the wheel, Jack stared straight ahead and said nothing. The Shadow Doctor took a deep breath before speaking.

'Jack, the way I spoke to you just now was inexcusable, and I am deeply, deeply ashamed. Earlier today I was pontificating about the folk we encounter being the most important people in the world. Now I behave as if I am allowed to decide who those people will be – as if there ever can be any exceptions.'

Jack lowered his forehead to the steering wheel. The mixture of hurt and embarrassment was overwhelming. Doc's bladed words about Sam had cut deep into him, but the last thing he wanted was to be one of the Shadow Doctor's customers. He most certainly did not want to be a squirming victim of compassionate restraint.

'I really don't . . .'

Doc raised a hand. 'Sorry, Jack, just let me get to the end of my furrow. The fact is, I've been on my own doing this . . . this stuff . . . for so long now that I've forgotten what it means to be vulnerable – accountable, if you like, to someone who's far enough inside my space to ask questions that search me. I think my toy-chucking outburst just now suggests a fear that the whole thing might fall apart if I'm forced to be a little more focused than I have been in the past. There is a great truth somewhere in the middle of all that uncertainty as well, as you'll see if, despite everything, you're still kind enough to put up with my short lecture on attitudes to the humble onion tonight or tomorrow, but here's the main point. If you decide to join me, and I sincerely want you to, it's going to happen again – me shooting my mouth off, I mean. Because – and I do hope you understand this – acknowledging that you, Jack, really are the most important person in the world is not just a matter of being nice to you: it's about letting you right into my world and dealing with whatever you chuck in my direction. And, though I say it with quite a lot of trepidation, I need you to do the same for me. Please don't hold back. Take me on. No one else does. No one gets the chance. The bottom line is, I believe that we need each other. But, as I said to you right at the beginning, there will be storms on the way.'

Jack eased his weight from the steering wheel and looked across at the Shadow Doctor. He was some way from knowing exactly what the other man was talking about, but he understood enough to experience a level of relief that quite shocked him.

'For one awful moment I thought you were going to do good to me and tick me off on your list. Honestly. I did.'

'I have no such wicked plans,' said Doc, a tired smile spreading across his face. 'Jack, are we OK for now?'

'I think so,' replied Jack. 'We're fine . . . for now.'

'I'm so glad. I really am. But look, as I was so spectacularly unpleasant to you, I hope you might forgive me if I attempt to make it up to you.'

'You don't have to do that. All right, go on then. What are we going to do?'

'If you agree, I would like to make it possible for you to experience a foretaste of heaven.'

'Now?'

'Right now. Well, quite soon. What do you think? Does it appeal?'

'I would love it . . . I think.'

'Good. Turn the silver monster round, and head back towards Robertsbridge.' He glanced at his watch. 'Meatloaf was wrong. Heaven definitely can't wait. Let's go.'

14

The Centipede

Jack popped the last fragment of sweet, papery peshwari naan into his mouth and sat back happily. New Spice was buzzing with lunchtime custom. They had been lucky to get a table without booking. The food had been exceptional, Jack's tandoori prawn dish a mouthwatering example of how it could and should be done. Doc was carefully setting down the glass that had contained his pint of Kingfisher lager. He smiled at the expression on his companion's face.

'Are you in heaven, Jack?'

'Almost. A worthwhile expenditure of our precious appetites, would you say?'

'Of course. My debt is paid – more than paid. You probably owe me some slack.'

The banter was a perfect dessert.

'I'll bear that in mind. Gosh, I'm full. We got through a lot of food, didn't we?'

'We did. I was thinking, Jack, this might be a good place to bring Sam and Chris when we go out for our evening.'

'Hats and all?'

'That will need a vote. It also occurs to me that I should probably point out to Sam that, as far as her fear of exploding is concerned, if the love doesn't get her the curry probably will.'

Jack sat up straight. 'You wouldn't say that to her, would you?'

'I would. I will. She'll laugh her socks off. Favourite shortcut, remember? Don't worry, Jack, the Marsh-Wiggle Club is going to be a great success. We'll throw the windows and doors of our clubhouse open. Lots of fresh air. Anything could happen.'

Invisible hands pushed Jack into asking an obtrusive question. He sounded like a troubled ten-year-old.

'Doc, does it matter that they're gay?'

The Shadow Doctor tilted his head and peered judiciously at the ceiling, apparently giving the question a great deal of thought.

'I shouldn't think so,' he replied at last. 'Indian restaurants are pretty relaxed these days. It'll be fine. By the way, you had one more question. Was that it?'

Shelve it.

'You know I didn't mean that. Never mind. No, my other question was about the lady with the BMW in the car park.'

'Oh, yes.'

'Well, first of all, why did you ask her how she was going to fill her time?'

Doc scratched his head. 'You know, this is a very odd business, Jack – working out why I do things, I mean. Now that I've banned myself from reacting like a petulant child, I really have to think about it.'

He tapped the table meditatively with his finger for a moment.

'It's something like this. When I meet someone – anyone at all – for the first time, I've got into the habit of concentrating really hard on what they say, and how they say it. Forgive me for repeating that mantra of mine, but if there really are no unimportant people in the world, then every single encounter might be important. That's what happened with Alice, your gran.

'When you and I met the BMW lady there was one thing that struck me. She said something about having an extra hour to fill. People are usually very glad to have unexpected free time. Why did a lady like her look and sound so negative about a chance to do whatever she liked? That's all it was. It was like seeing a tiny, scribbled notice attached to the signpost for an unimportant roundabout exit. If you happen to spot it, you follow it.'

He shook his head as if to jiggle his understanding into place.

'Goodness, this is hard work. It reminds me of that Katherine Craster poem, written back in the nineteenth century, the one about the centipede. It goes something like this:

> The centipede was happy, quite,
> Until the toad, in fun,
> Said, 'Pray which leg goes after which?'
> Which worked his mind to such a pitch,
> He lay distracted in the ditch
> Considering how to run.

'It's not quite so debilitating, Mr Toad, but it does feel a bit like that.'

Jack nodded. He had rather enjoyed Doc's act of self-deconstruction.

'And when you went over to speak to her, what was it that made her laugh? And why did she give you a hug as well? You promised to tell me later.'

'As you know full well, I certainly did not promise to tell you why she hugged me, and as I have no idea why she did that I'm not even going to try. She laughed out of a sort of relief, I think. I told her that I had experienced gut-wrenching bereavement myself, and asked her if she wanted the appalling news or the not-quite-so-appalling-but-not-far-off news. She opted to start with the former, so I told her that, however well you might learn to steer round it, the pain is forever. It waits like a shady mugger around corners on sunny days. Steering doesn't work with ambushes like that.'

'That must have cheered her up.'

Doc smiled resignedly. Jack assumed that both of them were replaying the layby conversation in their heads.

'Not at all, but she received it without flinching. Then she asked me what the not-quite-so-appalling news was. So I told her.'

'What did you say?'

'Sometimes shit is manure. That's what I said. That's when she laughed.'

'And that was it?'

'I asked her to tell me her husband's name. She told me his name was Joshua. They have no children.'

'Then she hugged you.'

'Yes.'

'Do you think she was a Christian?'

Doc toyed with a fork before replying. 'No idea. I wouldn't have said so, no.'

'Did you say anything about that?'

'No.'

'But you might never see her again.'

'Jack, it's very flattering of you to suggest that I am the only possible means by which human beings can come to faith, but if there is a God . . .'

'I didn't mean . . .'

'If there is a God, a being who has created an entire universe, it seems eminently possible to me that he might be able to arrange the next step in this lady's journey towards him without depending exclusively on further contributions from me.'

'I'm sorry. It's just that we were always taught not to waste opportunities to share the gospel. It's difficult to . . . you know . . . shake some things off.'

'I understand that, but all of us also have to learn not to mess up tiny little first stepping stones like the one we've been talking about by forgetting that every single person is different. There is absolutely no point in rushing people into some skinny act of assent when they are vulnerable, ill-prepared and simply not ready. I mentioned the centipede just now.'

'You did. In the little poem.'

'Just before we exit heaven, I'm going to tell you another story about a centipede that might clarify this whole issue for us. It's not my story, and I can't remember where I first heard it, but it does make a good point. Are you sitting comfortably?'

'Er, yes.'

'Then I'll begin – sorry, fossil memory. You won't remember *Listen with Mother*. This story is about a man called

Fred who wanted a talking pet, so he went to a local pet shop on Saturday afternoon and asked the proprietor what she had.

'"Well," said the woman, "the only speaking creature we've got at the moment is a centipede. Two pounds to you."

'The man paid for his centipede and took it home in a small enclosed box. By the following morning the new pet had not said a word. Fred was planning to go to church that Sunday evening, and he thought it would be nice if the centipede came with him. After breakfast he called out to the centipede in its little box.

'"Centipede, centipede! Would you like to come to church with me this evening?"

'Nothing. Not a word. He tried again at lunchtime. Same lack of response. Finally, ten minutes before setting off for church, Fred decided to have one more try.

'"Centipede!" he called. "I would really love you to be in church with me this evening. Will you come?"

'At last a small voice piped up from inside the box. "I heard you the first time, Fred. I'm just putting my shoes on . . ."'

The Shadow Doctor plucked the bill from its faux-leather wallet and beckoned a passing waiter.

'Some people take an awful long time to get their shoes on, Jack. Doesn't mean they won't make it in the end.'

Two minutes later, as the two men approached the X-Trail in the restaurant car park, Doc came to a sudden stop and pointed downwards.

'Shoelaces undone, Jack. Careful.'

Jack scrunched to a halt on the loose gravel surface and bent his head.

'No they're not. Why did you . . . ?'

Glancing up, he saw that Doc was already waiting by the car, innocently examining something in the far distance. Jack decided to forgive him. It had been a very good lunch.

15

The Mystery of the Onion

'Onion.'

Jack spoke the word firmly as he and Doc sat down to their morning coffee. The atmosphere in the cottage was as bright as the bar of early summer sunshine that lit up the surface of the ancient oak table in the kitchen. Yesterday's events and conversations seemed to have had a mellowing effect on the world in general.

'You said you were going to deliver your famous onion lecture for my benefit. I'm ready.'

Silence. Doc was gazing through the window, an expression of deep concentration on his face. Jack waited. Nothing. He decided not to give up.

'Well, are you going to do it or not?'

More silence. There was an air of such profound gravity in the Shadow Doctor's stillness and distance that Jack began to feel slightly alarmed. Perhaps it was some kind of self-imposed trance. What should he do? He leaned forward and raised his voice a little.

'Doc, did you hear what I said? What are you thinking about?'

'Naturally, I am thinking,' replied the other man, turning his face to Jack at last and enunciating his next two words with meticulous deliberation, 'about onions.'

'Good. Right.'

'You like to cook, don't you, Jack? How much do you value onions?'

Jack sighed. He was just beginning to understand and tentatively accept that, in the Shadow Doctor's view of the world, parallel straight lines can occasionally meet in an unofficial sort of way, but the process was less of a learning curve and more of a vertical ascent. An obscure fact bobbed to the surface of his memory.

'I don't value them as much as the ancient Egyptians. I seem to remember from the introduction to one of my cookery books that they more or less worshipped onions because they thought the general shape and all those concentric circles seemed like symbols of eternity, and that was before they started doing any actual cooking with them.'

The Shadow Doctor nodded solemnly.

'Mm, interesting, Jack. Most interesting. Eternity. Yes. And when it does come to the actual cooking, how important is an onion likely to be, in your experience?'

Distracted from the bewilderment of Doc's elliptical excursion, Jack became quite animated. 'Well, in everyone's experience, really. Onions bring out the taste in other foods. I can't imagine doing something like a casserole, for instance, without using onions. They magnify the flavour. Prevent it from being tasteless. And if you cook them for long enough they're beautifully sweet. Really tasty.'

'Right! Right.' Doc smacked the table with one hand. 'I shall go and look for one right now.'

Rising with sudden energy to his feet, he moved across to the larder, returning after a few seconds with a substantial red onion in one hand. Resuming his seat, he plonked the handsome, purplish object down on the table and indicated it with his forefinger.

'That, Jack, is an onion.'

Jack studied it.

'Yes, I know.'

'A fine example of the vegetable that you have been describing. Essential to most dishes, an enhancer of tastiness and flavour. A singularly worthwhile entity. An onion. Agreed?'

'Agreed. But what has this to do with . . .'

The Shadow Doctor raised a hand to interrupt.

'Jack, we were talking about discussion and investigation. Let us discuss and investigate this. What would happen if, tragically, you lost faith in your onion? What if you developed a need to investigate your onion in order to reassure yourself that it actually existed? What if you said to yourself, "I cannot bear the thought that my onion has no centre, no objective reality? I must take it to pieces and discover the beating heart of this wonderful creation that I value so highly?" Tell me, how would you set about that, Jack? How would you begin?'

'Er, I suppose I might peel a layer off.'

'Yes, you might. And what would that reveal?'

Jack looked helplessly around the room searching for inspiration. Nothing presented itself. A grizzled old countryman in a Victorian print received his glance of supplication with a scornful, outraged stare.

'Another layer, I suppose.'

'And after that?'

'OK, OK, I think I get the picture. I'd take layer after layer off until there were no more layers left – or rather, nothing but lots of bits of layers of onion.'

'Yes, and then, depending on the individual person you are, the way in which you have been uniquely formed, you might decide that your onion never did really exist. After all, when you took it apart it disappeared. There was no heart. No centre. And that might be true. But what a disaster if you then decided to give up using the non-existent onions that perversely continued to be readily available in every supermarket and greengrocer's in the country. An eternity of unnecessarily tasteless casseroles. The thing is, Jack, that you and I . . .'

Leaning across, the Shadow Doctor placed an elbow down on the table and lifted the red onion from its place, hefting it in his hand with thoughtful concentration, like a bowler measuring the weight of a cricket ball. Finally, he let it rest on his open palm, midway between Jack's face and his own. His tone was positively Shakespearean.

'You and I know that the joy of an onion is not primarily in how it is made, but in what it does. Read about onions. Investigate onions. Google onions. Dissect and discuss onions. Organise onion missions if you like. Write choruses about onions if you absolutely must. But we will never forget, will we, Jack, that because of its very nature, if and when you stick this bad boy in the pot, it will make everything else zing with flavour, and if it doesn't . . .'

He placed the vegetable into Jack's hand and closed the young man's fingers firmly around it.

'If it doesn't . . . if it doesn't, then regardless of anybody else's opinion, you and I will know, won't we, that whatever else this object is, it is definitely not being an onion.

'My rather defensive point is that, while I am well aware of the need to take apart and explain the way in which I respond to people, it is also important to avoid ripping it apart so comprehensively that it disappears altogether. Do you take my rather defensive point?'

'I do,' replied Jack, adding drily, 'but I have to say that, in my view, that particular disaster is not one that is likely to threaten us in the very near future. What do you think?'

'Drink your coffee and enjoy the sunshine,' said the Shadow Doctor.

16

Disappointed Victor

'How are you feeling today, Jack?'

Jack stretched and yawned luxuriously as he stepped down from the bottom of the stairs into the kitchen. He was feeling good. He had slept late. The queue of shadowy threats that commonly lined up to prevent sleep from coming quickly and easily had not turned up for their shift last night. Waking had been like a warm memory of better times, periods in his early life when mornings were a daily renewal of optimism. It almost made him want to cry. From the bedroom window he had shaded his eyes with one hand as he watched a multicoloured, pulsating sun begin its drying process on the rainsoaked forest. The branches of the trees were dripping with light.

The Shadow Doctor was seated comfortably at the kitchen table, a small pile of post lying in a pool of sunshine before him, an unopened letter in his hand.

'I'm good, thanks, Doc. Sort of uncomplicated and . . . well, OK. Sorry I'm down late. I slept so well. I think I must have forgotten what it's like to be completely comfortable.'

'Interesting. Someone in a book I read a while ago maintained that in the middle of the night we are all poets or babies. Make any sense to you?'

Jack smiled and shook his head. 'It might do if I knew what it meant. Sounds clever. I stayed in a house where there was a new baby once. She didn't sleep like a baby at all. Her mum had to get up to her at least three times. Needed feeding or changing, I expect.'

'Perhaps that's what it means. In the middle of the night we're either bawling our eyes out for something we need or we're blowing bubbles of creativity. Anyway, I'm really glad you slept well. There's no hurry today. Nothing planned – not by me, at any rate. Help yourself to breakfast. I've had mine. Coffee in the pot.'

He waved the letter that he was holding. 'In a minute I'd like to ask your opinion about something.'

Some of Jack's fragile peace slipped away as he dropped a slice of bread into the toaster and contemplated Doc's final comment. What was his opinion worth? He still found it very difficult to believe that a man like the Shadow Doctor could genuinely be interested in anything he had to say. The question he had asked himself many times sprang up afresh, provoking the same reflux of panic. Why on earth was he here in this solitary place with this singular person? If his only function was to play a sort of dull Watson to Doc's spiritually eccentric Holmes, what was the point? No wonder that queue of threats had taken the night off. Obviously they'd been tipped off that they wouldn't be needed. He decided to ask an irrelevant question to show that he was not bothered.

'Why did you give up with the chicken run at the back? Foxes? Rats? I can't imagine you starting something and not finishing it.'

'They were bantams, and I didn't start it,' replied the Shadow Doctor. 'Somebody else did. Not my sort of thing, really.'

As far as he could recall, Jack had never had a door slammed in his face, but that was how it felt. Bang! Don't go there.

He munched his toast and sipped his coffee in an uncomfortable silence. All he'd done was ask about the chicken run, for goodness' sake. He took longer wiping his mouth than necessary, dropped the scrunched-up square of kitchen roll onto his plate, and looked across at the other man. Doc was still holding the unopened envelope in one hand and tapping a brass letter-opener gently against his forehead with the other.

'Forgive me, Jack,' he said penitently. 'As I keep on saying to you, it's a long time since I've had anyone walking around inside my life. If you want to go back upstairs and then come down again as a client, you'll get much better treatment. How were you to know that I once suffered serious abuse at the . . . no, it wouldn't be hands, would it? Claws. That's it. Serious abuse at the feathered claws of a Grey Frizzle Pekin bantam. Come on. Please laugh a little. Most kind. Thank you.'

He drew a deep breath.

'I'll tell you what that was really about one day. Promise. If you stay, that is. In the meantime, are you going to give me the benefit of your opinion?'

Jack would have done anything. Maybe that fundamental fear of his really would go away one day. He was not a client. Not a client. He was someone who walked around inside his host's life. How weird that this knowledge should be so satisfying.

'Yes, of course. If you want.'

'OK. This letter is from a gentleman who wrote to me a fortnight ago. I wrote back almost immediately, and this is his response. I'd like to read you that first letter he sent, and then you tell me what you would have said to him. We'll compare that with what I wrote in return, and last of all we'll open the one that came this morning and see what he says. Is that all right with you?'

'I've lost track a bit. Too many letters. But yes, carry on.'

'Two seconds. They're in my desk upstairs. Make some more coffee.'

'So, here's the first letter I received from Victor Morton. Have a read and tell me what you think. Coffee's perfect, by the way.'

Doc passed three sheets of paper across the table. Jack leaned back in his chair and studied the script for a moment. You didn't see many handwritten letters nowadays. Gran's writing had been quite faint and ornate. Victor Morton's was square and practical looking, possibly the hand of a man who is accustomed to writing by hand on a regular basis. He settled back and began to read.

Dear Sir,

Forgive me for not using your name, but I don't know what it is. Actually, apart from the fact that you appear to be a doctor of some kind, I don't know anything about you. I hardly know why I am writing, but, as the Mastermind questioner on television so frequently announces, I have started, so I shall definitely finish. Incidentally, if you are a doctor of medicine, it is certainly not in that capacity that I am seeking a response from you. Nor do I expect any response at all unless there is something that you wish to say having read this letter. Simply to be heard by a person whom I shall probably never meet will, I think, be a help in itself.

In case you are interested, your number was given to me by a friend who is one of a small community of monks at Quarr Abbey, a Benedictine monastery on the Isle of Wight. He indicated that I might find it helpful one day. Over the years I have learned to trust him, and so, when I recently arrived at a crossroads in my life that is less of a hackneyed metaphor and more a junction from which a number of roads all lead into darkness and all bear signposts to mutually exclusive destinations, I decided to take his advice. Forgive me, I am not being deliberately obscure. I am sure you will understand what I am saying by the time I reach the end of this letter. I called the number given to me by my friend, and a very helpful person supplied me with an address that would, she promised, enable anything I wrote to you to be passed on without being opened, as long as my name appeared somewhere on the envelope.

I hope you are reading my letter now, and I especially hope that it is not a burden to you. I know about burdens. Thank you for giving me your time.

My name is Victor Morton, and I have been an Anglican priest since my mid-thirties, when I abandoned an accountancy career to train for the ministry. At the time I would have said that I felt a 'call' to make this significant change in my life. Perhaps I did. As the years pass these terms become like ice cubes – you can see through them, and they are very difficult to hold on to. I am now in my seventies, and retired. I live in a cottage between Lewes and a town called Hailsham in Sussex, just north of the Downs.

I resolved that I would write to you after one particular evening a fortnight ago. I can recall every moment and every feeling pertaining to that experience.

I was sitting at my roll-top desk, deliberately allowing the atmosphere of a very raw October evening to seep into my soul. I remember thinking that all the light there had ever been in the world seemed to have gathered itself into the cold incandescence of a perfectly circular sun that was just beginning its slide down behind the crest of a hill that we locals call Fennerley Beacon. Everything else was grey, the lifeless, defeated grey of yesterday's overcooked pork. I thoroughly dislike pork that is not prepared perfectly.

When I glanced at my watch I saw that it was three minutes after six, past the time when I usually switched Radio 4 on to hear the news. In fact, I hadn't bothered to do that for several days, not since hearing one particularly significant item of news during my last visit to the hospital. I had been told, with great sensitivity, and just the right amount of sympathy, that I was going to die. At the age of seventy-three some ugly, greedy thing is eating away at my insides, and apparently there is nothing that can be done. There is no appeal.

It struck me, as I sat there at my desk, how strange it was that in the past week I had felt only two extremes of emotion. Mostly a flat, featureless calm, as though I

had survived an air crash and was floating quietly in
untroubled waters, waiting for the next thing to happen.
After all, I was alive. Every now and then I would stare
at my hands and make these brown, mobile fingers of
mine bend and move to my command, something that a
dead man would never be able to do.

'Being alive,' I muttered curiously to myself once or
twice, 'is so not being dead.'

The other extreme was a sort of vomiting panic,
momentary but terrifying, a fear that my heart was
attempting to escape from my body before that silent
monster inside me could consume the essence of all that
I truly was. In those moments I was left feeling small
and tearfully bewildered. Some things had changed so
abruptly.

From the moment when that death sentence was
passed, for instance, I had not spoken to God. I think I
know why that was. Another fear. A deep dread of yet
again facing the wall of silence that for four decades I
had rationalised and tried to understand and preached
about and ultimately forgiven, when no other option
presented itself.

You may quite reasonably think it a ridiculous
thought, but the prioritising certainty of departure
from this life seemed to stand at my elbow like some
genie in a pantomime. Perhaps God would allow me
one golden wish. One prayer. One heartfelt plea. Must
not waste it. Very well, but what should that final plea
be? What did I, Victor Morton, want more than
anything else in the world? Healing? Well, yes, but, let
us be honest, that sort of thing so rarely happens, and if

*death was an unalterable plan the golden wish would be
wasted.*

*There needed to be a sign, something pointing out a
pathway to the true desire of my heart, and on this
bleak October evening it appeared. A book that I had
been reading earlier lay open on the desk in front of
me. One verse of a longer poem caught my eye. I
remember scanning the words over and over again in
silence. Eventually. I picked the book up and read them
aloud. I have rather prided myself on an ability to do
justice to poetry as a reader, but on this occasion my
voice broke a little as I reached the final, optimistic line.
These are the words I read:*

> And in a hollow church a hollow priest
> Dry and dusty as some jewelled chalice locked
>   away for safety and for ever
> Will sit and sigh and gather oddments, scraps of
>   truth
> Remnants of an old, forgotten dream
> Ideas and words like autumn leaves made brittle
>   by a year of death
> And by the scorching summer sun
> And feel once more so glad, and oh, so very, very
>   sad
> That those who delicately brush his sprinkled
>   fragments from their Sunday-best
> Will never hear the distant, panic-stricken
>   scream
> And Jesus will be born.

*I think I nodded my head slowly as I closed the book
and laid it to one side. The time had come. No calm.
No panic. I must talk to God. Funny how your mind
takes pictures, isn't it? I noticed that, as I began to
speak, that glowing disc in the distance was partly
obscured by a belt of charcoal-coloured cloud. Perhaps
I fancied that it was an impressionist reflection of my
life. As far as I can recall, this is what I said:*

*'God, Father, Lord – forgive me, but after all these
years I really am not sure what to call you. I think I
shall call you Father, because that is what I most want
you to be. First of all, I want to thank you, whether you
exist or not, for all that my troubled relationship with
you has brought me over the years. I have enjoyed so
many things. So many good times with the folk who
trusted me with their failures and successes and doubts
and certainties. Lots of laughter. Many tears. A great
deal of togetherness. I have been told quite often that
an inner stillness and confidence in my dealings with
troubled souls has allowed them to gain the small foot-
hold necessary to clamber back up to the cliff edge of
peace. What more could I ask? What indeed?*

*'You, if you are here and listening to me now, know
the truth. Almost always that stillness and confidence
has actually been a silence of incomprehension and
swirling inadequacy. I have gradually learned to be still.
I have learned how to listen. I have understood that the
rescuing of lost souls requires me to place one foot in
the ditch where they have fallen, and the other solidly
on the bank so that they may feel safe. Thank you for
all that, especially if you bypassed my crashing silence*

so that bruised and broken hearts could begin to be healed. But did you? Were you there?

'Forgive me if this sounds disrespectful or ungrateful, but, looking back, I see that I was involved in many, many meetings, encounters, events, all sorts of things where the only person who failed to turn up was you – or so it seemed.

'Now I am going to die, and I want to tell you this. Despite everything, I have always loved the you that is either there or not there. Tears fill my eyes as I speak. You. You producer of silence – you have been my passion. But all the prayers I have said throughout my life, all the words of praise or worship that have ever passed my lips, come together now in one final request. One last plea. As the sun sinks slowly on my life in this world, please promise that you will do one thing for me. I can sum it up in a single word.

'Be.

'Let Jesus be born again in the scruffy stable of my soul.

'Please be.'

So, Shadow Doctor, whoever you may be, that was my request to God on that morning, and it continues to be my only prayer. So far my request has not been granted. My prayer remains unanswered, at least as far as I can see. I would offer such wonderfully wise counsel to myself if I was able to split the priest from the petitioner, but that is a metaphysical step too far. The words I have offered to others in the past lie before me like a sheet of bubble wrap. The little air pockets go pop as soon as I apply pressure to them. Once they lose

*their power to afford protection, they are worth
nothing.*

*Time is short. Thank you so much for listening. I know
it is pure pie-in-the-sky conjecture, especially as we have
never met, but I think that we might have been friends.*

Yours very sincerely

Victor.

Replacing the sheets in their correct order, Jack passed
Victor Morton's letter back across the table. Pulling the last
sheet away from the kitchen roll, he dried his eyes carefully
before attempting to speak.

'Sorry, it was a bit upsetting. I feel so . . . so very sorry
for him. It's unbearably sad to think that, after a life of
giving out to others, he has to end up with it all feeling,
well, so dismal. So thin.'

'I found it upsetting.' Pause. 'What do you think you
might have said to him in reply?' The Shadow Doctor's face
gave nothing away.

Jack considered.

'I'll tell you what I might have said until I came here and
met you and . . . and things began to look different.'

'OK. Tell me that.'

Jack mentally surveyed the array of knee-jerk responses
that had popped up like unwanted adverts on a PC screen in
the course of reading Victor Morton's letter. It interested
and slightly shocked him to observe and feel the angst-
ridden nature of those reactions. Fear, panic, a strange,
corporate defensiveness on behalf of the whole Christian
edifice, a frantic need to rearrange and restate the problem
that had been expressed before it got out of hand and

attacked and engulfed his own fragile stability – all of those things had been present. It was a forest that he had fought his way through many times in the past. Trying to help others by bashing out paths that didn't really exist. Cutting and slashing at tangled undergrowth to create a temporary clearing. These battles had earned him a measure of gratitude and respect, but not from himself, and there was an issue of authenticity that he had never allowed himself even to think of in those terms.

'I suppose I might have pointed out how wonderful his ministry sounded, how many people must have reason to be very, very grateful for all the support and comfort he's brought into their lives. I would probably have said that just because you're not conscious of the presence of God, it doesn't mean that he isn't there. I would have assured him that God would answer his prayer eventually, and undoubtedly I would have pointed out that God's timing is always perfect. What else? Promised to pray, of course. Worried that I wouldn't. Possibly put a Bible verse at the bottom.' He heaved a sigh. 'I think that's about it.'

The Shadow Doctor nodded, then leaned his chair back dangerously on two legs, supporting his weight with a hand on the edge of the work surface behind him. With his other hand he fished out a new kitchen roll from the cupboard under the sink, regained equilibrium, and threw the roll with pinpoint accuracy into Jack's lap.

'What would you say now?'

Jack burst into tears.

Several sheets of kitchen roll later, his unexpected outpouring reduced to a slight sniff, he had calmed sufficiently to attempt an answer to Doc's question.

'I would tell him that the things he wrote made me cry. I would tell him that I was frightened and panicked by his fear and panic. I would tell him how desperately inadequate his letter made me feel because I can't think of a single thing to say that comes anywhere close to being helpful. I would tell him that the best I could offer would be me popping round with a bottle or two of something so that he and I could be happily miserable together. I'd tell him I hope from the bottom of my heart that God will answer his prayer in the way he wants, although nobody in the world can guarantee it. I would tell him how sorry I am that he's so poorly and unhappy.' Sniff. 'That's what I'd say. True, but pretty useless.'

The Shadow Doctor slid another sheet of paper from the folder in front of him.

'Do you want to know what I said when I replied?'

'I can't begin to imagine,' said Jack wearily. 'Scrabble? Crossword clue? Sharing the information that stealing apples is the worst sin you can possibly commit? A lecture on onions? Could be anything. Bound to be something I never expected. Yes, all right, I would like to know. You know I want to know. I know you know I want to know.' He waved a hand, dismissing his own burblings. 'Go on. Read it to me.'

Doc received Jack's list with raised eyebrows and a broad smile. 'I'm flattered. I hadn't realised I was so versatile. OK, this is a copy of my letter to Victor. I'll read it to you. Here we go.

Dear Victor,
    It is unutterably sad to hear that you have turned your back on one of the greatest providers of comfort

and support that a human being can experience. I refer,
of course, to your abandonment of Radio 4. I know for
a fact that God is a regular listener, especially to The
Archers. Occasionally, I gather, as in the current, tragic
case of Rob and Helen, he intervenes. Also, of course, I
always listen to Melvyn Bragg. Promise that your return
to faith will begin with a strong resolve to join me in
this act of commitment. Victor, let your model of deter-
mination be drawn from God himself. After he had
toiled hard for the first twenty-four hours of creating
this world, did he say, 'I think I'll call it a day'? No, he
did not – well, actually, he did, of course, but you know
what I mean . . .

My friend, I drivel on like this because I came very
close to chickening out of writing back to you. You
have obviously dealt with just about every problem I
can imagine, and quite a few I've never heard of. In fact,
there's nothing I can say about your situation that you
haven't said yourself to some poor soul in the past. All
the traditional responses are going to sound very
hollow. Your ice-cube/bubble-wrap metaphors just
about sum it up. The more I read, the more depressed I
became. My instinct is always to look for windows,
doors, skylights, air vents, any sort of way through to
the merest hint of a beginning of a solution. There
usually is one. Not this time. You are going to die, and
the God you have tried to serve for so long is simply not
putting in an appearance. I can't make him do what you
want. I wish I could. I am in the dark and I have noth-
ing to offer except for a willingness to be with you in
your darkness in as far as that is possible.

I will continue to ask and search for that way through, but I cannot begin to think what it could possibly be. You write very entertainingly, by the way. I am not patronising you in the least when I say that I like the sound of the inside of your head. I think I would have enjoyed your sermons. Forgive my helplessness. By the way, if you would like a short visit, I drive along that bit of the A27 every now and then on my way to Lewes. You're only about forty minutes from us.
   Yours very sincerely,
Doc

P.S. I am enclosing a piece written from the perspective of a man who finds himself in a situation similar to your own. Just another shout of pain. Read it or bin it, or both.

Jack was nonplussed. The sentiments expressed in the letter certainly echoed his own, far more closely than he would have expected, in fact, but apart from the first part of the letter the tone seemed bleak to the point of harshness. He was accustomed to Doc dealing with problems and personalities in his own unpredictable way, but the Shadow Doctor always seemed to come up with something original and effective. Not on this occasion. Nothing for Victor Morton. How would the suffering clergyman deal with a paragraph of flippancy and a page of negativity?

'What do you think?' Doc was irritatingly impassive.

Jack shook his head in bewilderment. Truth or imprisonment?

'If you must know, I thought your letter was a bit depressing. Couldn't you have been just a tiny bit encouraging?'

The Shadow Doctor pursed his lips. 'I couldn't think of anything encouraging to say, Jack. I certainly wasn't going to make something up.'

'What if he takes up your offer of a visit? Have you got something in mind to say to this poor gentleman?'

'Nothing at all. I like your suggestion, though. I might take a bottle of wine with me. Or two. That's what you said, isn't it? Anyway, shall we open this letter and find out what he said?'

'Go ahead. Read it.'

'OK.'

Doc sliced the envelope with the letter-opener and withdrew a sheet of paper. A smile touched his face as he silently scanned the first few lines. Looking up, he caught Jack's eye and began to read out loud.

Dear Doc,

I wish to thank you most sincerely for two great gifts that I have received through your recent letter. First, and most important, of course, is your gentle rebuke concerning Radio 4. I have recently found myself sensing an aura of hurt and disappointment in the very air that surrounds my Roberts Classic DAB set. 'Why,' it seemed to be saying, 'do we no longer turn each other on?' Your words opened my deafened ears to the depth of need expressed in this sad plea. Now, I am thrilled to say, a reconciliation has taken place. Doc, we are listening to each other. I feel a cleaner, better person altogether.

Regarding your comments on the aridness of my present situation, I must be honest and say that your straightforwardness caused me to weep a little, mainly with relief. Ever since I learned that my days are numbered, specifically or randomly, depending on whether there is a God or not, I have dreaded and avoided those who are likely to offer me human optimism, or compassionately fuelled words from God, or anecdotal indications that all is not necessarily lost. Your commitment to the truth adds some welcome scaffolding to my miniscule store of hope. Thank you for that, and, if you have any spare time, please continue to hunt for the items you mention in that fascinating list of exits and entrances. I feel quite confident that you would never offer me anything that has not been given to you.

If you really mean it, I would love a visit, however brief. Dare I be vulnerable enough to say that I yearn for someone to hold my hand, just for a few seconds? Like that small child I once read about, I need God with skin on at the moment. I'll show you my view if you come.

Yours sincerely, and so much less than my name,
Victor

P.S. Later on this evening I intend to re-read the piece you sent. Would I be entirely wrong in suspecting that this is your work? You did write it, didn't you?

'You will go, won't you?' Jack was almost pleading.

'Yes, I will drop in as soon as I can.'

'Could I come?'

'Of course, if you'd like to.'

'What shall we take with us?'

'Us.'

'Doc, this thing you sent to Victor – he says you wrote it. Did you?'

The Shadow Doctor placed both hands on his head and leaned sideways out of his natural spotlight. 'Yes, I did, but it's just . . . it's nothing.'

'Can I see it?'

'There's a copy on my desk in a thin blue folder. It's just . . . look, it's nothing, Jack, honestly.'

'I'll read it now.'

Jack found the folder, clattered back down the stairs, and pulled a kitchen chair out into the morning sunshine. Before opening the folder he thought about Victor for a moment. Later today the retired vicar would be reading exactly the same words. From the bottom of his heart, Jack prayed that it would help in some way. He lifted the blue cover and began to read.

17

A Tiny Patch of Blue

There is only one constant. Pain. There is only one preoccupation. Pain. There is only one message from the whatever to the whoever. Pain. Pain tears me. Pain eats me. Pain defeats me.

So why not leave me alone with this consistently attentive, hungry companion of mine? You, who see no problem when it comes to cashing in the chips of love. You, who have pushed and led and coaxed me all my life along the dry and dusty road to something that may or may not actually exist on the other side of darkness. How is it that your still, small voice insists on breaking through this ugly crust of agony to speak sweet words of power into a world that has refused to hear my voice, and kills my racked and wretched body inch by inch?

Yes, I heard him. Heard the two of them. The things they said. Of course I did. And finally I heard the strangled words of hopeless hope that whispered from the cracking lips of one who knew that I had done no wrong, never had deserved these nails, this pain.

Would I remember him?

And out came the words. The words have always come. My mouth moved. My mouth has always moved. My heart knows the script. My heart has always known the script. And yet it never was a script of words. More like some kind of humble sieve through which the purest elements of love or justice have to pass, nothing more, and never ever less.

'Yes – truly – this day – you will be with me – paradise.'

I saw the miracle again, the miracle of mere imagination gaining shape and colour and reality. I saw a particle of hope appear upon that ravaged face, hope like the tiniest patch of blue in skies that have been black with storm clouds. He believed me. At any rate, he believed you.

But now I have to ask you something. What of the sieve? What of the broken, useless, worn-out sieve? What of me? Do I believe me? Do I believe this talk of paradise? The comfort that I offered. Does it comfort me? Those words of life and hope and dreams that might come true, they fill the part of me that you inhabit. Yes, they always did. But now the child in me, the carpenter's child in me, is longing, crying, for his home in Nazareth, his mother with her watchful eye, his devoted, puzzled father, his friends, so funny, flawed and faithful, for Bethany, a place of love and food and blessed ordinariness. That bewildered child weeps for them and wishes that he could be back there now.

Why have you forsaken me? Why have you gone? Why are you somewhere else? Why have you turned your face away from me as though I was the one who broke your heart? I never did. I always walked with you. You know I did. I always listened. Always took the greatest care to speak the words you placed into my keeping.

I remember – how could I forget? – the shining day on which you spoke to me from heaven, called me your beloved son, said that you were proud of me. I was clothed in affirmation and approval. Warmed into obedience, not through duty, not through dull require-ments of law, but because your love was greater than my weakness or my fear.

So why have you forsaken me? Why have you forsaken me? I have never forsaken you. I have done my aching best, my very best for every hour of every day of my short life. Why have you forsaken me? Why? Why am I alone and cold and suffocated in my spirit by a sobbing fear that this, my final act of sacrifice, will pay the price and save the world, but leave me in the wilder-ness for ever?

I do not want this. I do not want to be forsaken. What do I want? I want to sit with Peter by the fire, when all the rest have gone off yawning to their beds. I want to listen to his talk of nets and fish, and chuckle at the silly things he did when he was young. And yet . . .

Gethsemane.

The trees. The night. The fireflies. You and me. The others all asleep.

I was very nearly crushed by grief, could hardly breathe. I had to ask the question. Just in case. Just in case. Just in case there was another way. And when the answer came, that sorrowing silence of an answer, something seemed to set like steel inside me. Tears, fears, the pain and passion of the years, folded, packed and placed aside. Too heavy for this journey. And at that moment I was sure because you were so sure, and that is why you leave me with no choice. That is why you leave me. That is why. That.

There is only one constant. Pain. There is only one preoccupation. Pain. There is only one message from the whatever to the whoever. Pain. Pain tears me. Pain eats me. Pain defeats me. But soon it will be finished. Then I will know. I will know why you have forsaken me.

Hope. A tiny patch of blue in stormy skies. I wait. I wait in pain. I was obedient, and so I have no choice.

18

Back to the Future

Jack busied himself making hot chocolate. Doc placed two kitchen chairs in front of the oven's open twin doors and lit the gas, turning it up high once the flame was established. It was the easiest, quickest, most expensive way to produce effective heat on such a freezing cold night. Still encased in their overcoats, the two men sat in an uneasy, huddled silence for a while, clasping their mugs with both hands and staring wide-eyed into the oven as though they were watching something deeply absorbing on a TV screen. Neither broke the uneasy silence.

'Why were you so frightened down there in the forest just now?'

Silence again. To Jack it seemed to go on for ever. He wanted to help. He didn't want to break into the very centre of the other man's world unless he really was wanted there. This was new territory. He felt no desire to solve problems. He just wanted to be in it with his friend. He passionately wanted that. Since the moment when the Shadow Doctor had suddenly realised he was not alone in the forest, he had said only one word.

'Jack!'

After that, as the two men trudged their way back to the house, Jack had stumblingly tried to explain that he had been hovering on the edge of sleep when sounds of the other man getting up and creaking his way down the wooden stairs had brought him fully awake. A few moments later, hearing a jingle of keys and the front door opening down below his window, he had thrown some clothes on and followed Doc into the forest, just in time to see him duck down and away from the path towards the clearing.

'You must have left the house unlocked, then. Otherwise I would have heard.'

This uncharacteristically graceless response was all that Jack heard from the Shadow Doctor until they regained the cottage. It filled him with misery. The misery persisted, but Jack was determined to ask the obvious question, however nerve-racking the prospect of getting or not getting a reply. Until now, in his eyes at least, the Shadow Doctor had appeared to live such a very controlled life within himself for most of the time, filled with all kinds of rich, strange and surprising things, usually released in a measured, almost stylised way. But the raw components of his personality and state of mind were rarely expressed or made available. His past was a far country that Jack had not yet summoned up the courage to explore. There was a power of contained passion in the man that silently resisted intrusion.

Jack found the courage to repeat his question.

'Can I ask you – why *were* you so frightened down in the woods just now? I heard you cry out. I mean – I'm frightened by lots of things, but I've never thought of you as the sort of person who gets scared. What I mean is, what are you so scared of? You don't have to tell me. Would you like me to make some toast?'

Blushingly aware that he had started to burble, Jack half rose from his chair, but sank back again as the Shadow Doctor smilingly made a calming motion with one hand.

'No, no toast for me, thanks. Nice hot chocolate. Most people make it too weak. You have to be bravely extravagant with the stuff . . . the powder, don't you?' He took another sip from his mug. 'This is just right. I will try to tell you what I'm scared of, Jack. I'm a little surprised to find that I'd really like to. I think it might be a good idea.'

Jack was surprised and disturbed to find a tangled jungle of his own fears thrusting intrusively penetrating fronds into his consciousness at that moment. It required an effort of will to dismiss this rush of self-absorption so that he could concentrate on what the other man was about to say.

Doc was staring at him.

'If you really want to hear, that is.'

He knows, thought Jack. Blow the man! He can see the jungle. He looks right into me. Hold your nerve. You're living on the same island.

'Of course I do.'

Turning his head, the older man continued to stare fixedly into the depths of the oven, the slight flickering of the blue and orange gas flames reflected in his eyes as he collected his thoughts. Jack found himself silently recalling a few words from an old Louis Armstrong classic. Something about the dark sacred night. He sensed that this was a conversation that was unlikely to happen again.

The Shadow Doctor cleared his throat.

'Before I start, Jack, please would you be kind enough to forgive my unpleasant remark about locking the house on the way up just now. I was embarrassed. A good thing in a way. Quite a relief, in fact. Doesn't happen much nowadays. It suggests that I'm at least halfway sane.'

Jack was deeply embarrassed by Doc's embarrassment. 'Of course I forgive you,' he mumbled.

'Thank you. I mean it. OK. Tonight, Jack, I was terrified and exhausted by my part in a battle that was beginning to look as if it might be lost. Ultimately, I don't believe that it has been lost, not for now at any rate, but it was an experience of hellish darkness, and I never want to go there again.' He checked before continuing. 'I would . . . I hope I will go there again if it's asked of me.'

He paused, a tightly contained shiver running almost imperceptibly through the length of his body.

'I will tell you more about that in a little while, but that is only one of my fears – the current one. The ongoing list is quite long. Where shall I start? OK – I'm scared, like a famous man whom you will have read about and discussed many times, of taking one more failing step on the surface of the water.'

He scratched his head ruefully.

'Passion and courage and raw desire can precipitate us into taking a single step into the land of miracle, especially when we don't think about it too much. But the thought of the second step, the step that truly, drastically alters our whole way of life, our very selves – that is the prospect that can drain the life from me. If the bridge across the chasm remains invisible until I risk death by stepping into the abyss, I will always be tempted to opt for the delusion of safety. Narrow gate, difficult path. Always was. Always will be. All that.'

He thought for a moment.

'Have you ever watched one of those old black-and-white Laurel and Hardy films, Jack?'

Jack shrugged, shook his head blankly, and said nothing.

'Stan was skinny and not very bright. Olly was fat and usually cross with Stan. They both wore bowler hats. Very famous in their time. There's one of their films that always gave me the shivers. Stan and Olly have to deliver an upright piano from one side of a deep canyon to the other. The only way across is a crazily narrow, swinging horror of a rope-bridge with no handrails. Goodness knows how they filmed it. My nightmare is that I find myself faced by that same bridge, and at the far end there's a huge, uncompromising sign in big red capital letters that simply says "THIS WAY". The problem, you see, is that knowing the right way doesn't necessarily take away the fear. I can see exactly where the next part of the journey needs to take me. There it is – just over there. The other side of the canyon. Simple, isn't it? Except that it's not. I don't know if you will understand this, Jack, but I am scared of the very things I want, because I have a feeling I can only have those things if I give up the right to be absolutely sure that they exist, and any certainty of ever safely reaching or finding them. '

Jack wanted to say something, almost anything to prove to himself that he was in the same room. His voice emerged as little more than a whisper.

'Would that be something to do with faith – or lack of faith?'

Doc made a twisting, impatient movement with his head and shoulders. 'I suppose you could fold up all that I've just said and pack it neatly away in that little word, Jack, but why would I . . . why would anyone want to do that?'

Jack had banked a substantial deposit of frustration and bewilderment since his first encounter with the Shadow Doctor. Some of it spilled out of him now.

'But that's just it! That's exactly what's beginning to get on my nerves. You don't want to give anything a name, do you? Nothing. What is it? Are you worried that if you call something what it is, it won't exist any more?'

Jack dropped the top half of his body forward, hands clasped over the top of his head, then surfaced abruptly and swung round, hands spread apart, begging for an answer to his question. The other man shook his head rapidly and rhythmically, apparently working to control some strong emotion. Jack tried once more.

'Well, come on. Is that it? Is that what you're worried about?'

For a few moments Doc was still, his head raised and tilted, as though he was listening. Then, quite suddenly, all his tension seemed to relax and escape into a deep sigh. When he turned to Jack there was a smile of resignation on his face. It was a good smile, crinkly and warm.

'Jack, thank you so much once again for reminding me that you are here to do me good, not just by sharing my love for people and fine whisky and changes in the weather, but by challenging me as well. You are absolutely right. I am indeed worried about using important words that have all but lost their meaning through continual disuse. In the past I have felt my . . . hold on, should I say this? Yes, because it's true, and important to me. If we really are going to work together, I must do my best to help you understand.

'There was a time in my life when things went very badly for me for a number of reasons. I might tell you more about that one day. For now, I just want to tell you about one of those reasons – those triggers. I know this will sound a tad melodramatic, but I could feel my spirit being crushed by the sheer weight of meaninglessness. And a lot of that was to do with the way in which meaning and depth seemed to be dumped by the wayside, and replaced with words – or labels, if you like. It drove me mad. It made me want to put my hands over my ears and crouch down in a corner to get away from the babel. I didn't actually do much of that because I would rather work with a fountain pen than be supplied with a nice, safe crayon in an institution. But I did get a bit peculiar. Still am, I expect.'

He paused, looking enquiringly into the young man's eyes. 'Jack, before I go on, do you have the faintest idea what I'm talking about?'

Jack nodded his head solemnly three times before saying, with equal solemnity, 'No. Actually, I really, really do not.'

'Ah, well, why don't you pour us a small Lagavulin each and I'll try to make it clear.' As Jack disappeared towards the sitting room, he leaned his head back and called out, 'Bring the bottle in case we want another small one afterwards, and shut the door while you're out.'

The confined kitchen was warming up remarkably quickly. After Jack made his shivering, clinking return with bottle and glasses, both men shed their coats and scraped their chairs back a little from the heat. The Shadow Doctor rested an arm across the kitchen table and gazed reverentially at his drink.

'OK, just imagine, Jack,' he said, 'that I've invited you to my house and I'm showing you around, pointing out all my stuff. "Look," I say, pointing to a truly dreadful, awful painting on the wall, "isn't that a wonderful piece of work? If you don't believe it, just read the label." And, sure enough, there's a yellow Post-It slip stuck to the bottom of the frame. Someone has written the words "FINE ART" on the slip. Everything in my house is the same. A horrible, battered old packing case in the middle of the living room is labelled "ANTIQUE OCCASIONAL TABLE", the "PERSIAN RUG" that it stands on is a grubby piece of sacking, and the Post-It saying "BIRD OF PARADISE" is sellotaped on the side of a cage that houses a rather embarrassed fly-blown little blue budgie. If you try to argue with me I simply point out the legends in capital letters on the bits of sticky paper. And anyway, it's my house, my rules, my labels, my stuff, my game. Take it or leave it. Or leave.'

Jack was smiling now.

'You've thought about this, haven't you?'

'Just a little.' Doc took another lingering sip from his glass. 'It got ... still gets like that in church circles. "WORSHIP" is singing, broadly speaking. "CONFESSION", at its grinding worst, is a miserable, one-sided conversation with an invisible god who, it is hoped, will stop holding his nose as soon as the statutory passwords have been mumbled. "FOLLOWING JESUS" is assembling a set of principles that are greater obstacles to the work of God than any mere sins will ever be. "PRAYER" can be anything from a collection of hollow mantras to a sort of bouncing neurosis, a depressed yearning that's got itself recycled and cranked up into something that feels like contact with the supernatural.

'Then there's "THEOLOGY AND THE STUDY OF SCRIPTURE". I'm reminded of a man I once knew who had taken his car to pieces in the yard behind his house, and never quite got round to putting it together again. It was a hobby and a relaxation that he enjoyed enormously, and he had probably become seriously expert in just about every aspect of vehicle maintenance. Sadly, though, and clearly rather oddly, he was unwilling or unable to bring himself to actually drive the car. I got the feeling he was a bit nervous of traffic. His wife, who knew nothing about mechanics, drove her car very happily all over the place. The same applies to some of the churches I've known where a large percentage of the available time is spent desperately trying to work out how to turn the church into whatever they thought it ought to have been in the first place. Are you beginning to get my drift, Jack?'

'Do you mean they fix whatever they think is wrong with the church, rather than doing what Jesus told us to do?'

A confirming nod.

Uneasily, but with unaccustomed assurance, Jack was experiencing a shift of consciousness. He was not supposed to swallow everything that the Shadow Doctor said, not without exercising his own freedom to respond.

'I'm sorry, but I don't understand some of the things you've said. How can principles get in the way of following Jesus?'

'I'm talking about human principles, Jack. People are so relieved when they feel they've sorted out a list of the things they always do and the things they never do, the people they disapprove of and the ones who are OK because their moral compass happens to be set in exactly the same direction.'

'But I still don't see . . .'

'Loyalty to your friends is a wonderful principle, wouldn't you say, Jack?'

'Yes, of course.'

'So, when your beloved friend tells you that he's embarking on a course that will end in death or disaster, and you know that you could save him from that fate, you would do anything to help. Is that right?'

'Yes . . . yes, I would . . . I mean, I hope I would. Yes, that is right.'

'Suppose, when you tried to express those passionate feelings to your friend, he were to turn and angrily accuse you of representing the devil in his life?'

'You're talking about . . .'

'I'm talking about the essential being sacrificed to moral impulses that take no account of a picture that may be bigger and more necessary and more far reaching than any of us can imagine. Jack, it's a place of inner conflict that might cause the strongest and most committed person to weep with the pain of having to choose between the immediate needs of friends and the central reason for their existence. It certainly made one man weep.'

Everything in Jack wanted to make sure that he had understood what lay at the still centre of the Shadow Doctor's swirling words. Was he talking about the shortest verse in the Bible? Would it seem obvious and a bit silly to ask? Probably. Change the subject. Be assertive about something else.

'If you don't mind me saying so, you seemed very scathing about prayer.'

'I don't mind you saying so in the slightest, and I'm quite sure I did sound scathing. I feel angry and frustrated by the nonsenses that are peddled under that particular heading, and I am equally sure that my attitude is seriously in need of a moderating influence.'

He gave Jack a very straight look.

'Fancy the job?'

A yawning chasm of inadequacy seemed to open up before Jack's feet. How was he, a confused, insubstantial excuse for a human being, going to exercise any kind of moderating influence on someone like the Shadow Doctor, a man who was more multilayered, complex and strangely confident than anyone he had ever known?

What is the problem with prayer?

'Doc, what is the trouble with prayer?'

'The trouble with prayer? Nothing much. Only that it doesn't work.'

The reply caused a sensation in Jack that was very akin to physical pain. It was impossible simply to switch off an inbuilt mechanism that for years had been driving him mercifully or mercilessly into devising a solution to any problem that that was presented to him. Doc's statement was as blunt and coldly penetrative as a bullet. The words bled from him.

'Don't you think that's rather dishonouring to God?'

The Shadow Doctor punched a fist solidly into the palm of his other hand, resting his chin for a moment on his clasped hands before raising his eyes and addressing Jack in the voice of a man who is finally being allowed to get something off his chest.

'But does it come within a gnat's whisker of dishonouring God as much as all our lamentably common attempts to find shallow safety and reassurance in a spiritual philosophy based on coincidence or relying on exaggeration, or rationalising disappointment or disaster? How do you think this same God – assuming he exists – feels about having his deficiencies shored up and explained away by those of us who can't survive without straight lines and mechanically predictable outcomes? It's a nonsense. It's a distracting nonsense. It's stubborn resistance to the clearest nonsense of all. The nonsense about prayer. It doesn't work.'

Jack knew that his face had become flushed. The heat was like a fever. He could hardly contain the surge of passion in his chest that he supposed must be something close to pure anger. But anger doesn't solve problems. Or does it? In this new territory – it might. He pushed his symbolic whisky glass even further away across the table, raising his extended hand and pointing a rigid finger directly into Doc's face.

'OK, I get what you're saying – or I think I do. Lots of us go wrong when it comes to prayer, and yes, I expect you're right. We probably don't do God any favours by inventing things to make ourselves feel better. But the fact is that I simply don't believe what you've just said. And I know exactly what's going to happen next. You'll probably rant on like that for another five minutes, and then you'll do one of your sudden magic U-turns and start raving on about how wonderful prayer is after all. Except that now you're the one who's allowed to talk about what prayer really, really means, and we have to abide by the very special revelation that you are kind enough to offer us poor, deluded Christian misfits. You want to own the problem and the solution. You want to be in charge, as long as you don't have to take responsibility for actually changing anything.'

Jack lowered his forefinger, angrily tapping the table each time he made a point.

'You *do* believe that prayer works! I *know* you do! You just won't *say* it!'

Jack slumped the top half of his body onto the table, exhausted by his own outspokenness, but the Shadow Doctor appeared totally unmoved by the younger man's passionate outburst. He nodded slowly in the subsequent silence, and after a moment or two of thoughtful consideration, replied quietly and calmly as though their conversation had been conducted in the mildest possible manner.

'I receive all that you say. However, the fact remains that prayer does not work. I tried it a couple of weeks ago, for instance. I asked God very politely if he would be kind enough to take the rubbish down to the end of the drive for me – a task I really dislike, as you know. I then sat back here in the kitchen with my eyes closed waiting to hear the sound of the bins rumbling along – just to be sure that the job was getting done, you understand. Well, I didn't hear a thing – not a solitary rumble. And when I went outside to check, the bins were exactly where I'd left them. Why? I don't know. Perhaps God was no keener on messing about with the trash than I was.'

He seemed to warm to his theme.

'My friend's little son Alfie had a similar problem. His dad had told him that the creator of the universe was interested in every little thing in our lives, and that we should go straight to God if we need anything. Alfie was off school the next day with a bug, and when he first woke in the morning feeling weak and woozy he asked God, perfectly nicely I'm sure, if he would be kind enough to draw the curtains for him. The curtains remained closed until God's agent on earth, Alfie's mother, arrived on the scene.

'Naturally, Alfie was scandalised. Such a trivial favour to ask. Surely all it required was one novice angel with a basic understanding of the need to bring light into darkness? Bread-and-butter stuff for a heavenly being, one would have thought.'

Jack leaned back and took a breath, but the Shadow Doctor was really motoring now.

'Actually, now that I think about it, lots of my prayers haven't been answered over the years. World peace, for instance. That's something I've been going on about for some time whenever I've got a moment to spare. An end to war in Afghanistan was another, more specific request. That could have been done and dusted very satisfactorily way back when the conflict first began if God had decided to stretch the muscles of his much-vaunted omnipotence in response to one of my prayerful suggestions.

'Poverty all over the world, starvation, suffering, mistreatment of children, natural disasters, all avoidable if Alfie's father had been right, and God had been prepared to live up to his reputation.

'Honestly, it is a bit off, don't you think? And, to make matters worse, when you express these very reasonable complaints to other believers they tend to come out with the tired old rationalisations that I mentioned just now, as well as loads of pet schemes for making prayer easier or more enjoyable. I wouldn't particularly want it to be more enjoyable, and I'm bored to tears by hearing that the reply to any prayer might be "Yes" or "No" or "Wait". And yes, just in case you bring it up, I know all about the thing you do with your fingers where the index finger is pointing at other people, and the smallest finger is the one pointing back at ourselves – ah, see what you're doing there – and the thumb and the other two fingers point to some other categories of people or institutions that I can't remember for the life of me. Then there's that exercise they do out there in obscure bits of Europe, where you breathe Jesus in with one breath and breathe him out with the other. Can't do it. My head goes funny.

'I could go on. I will go on. Writing sins on bits of paper and burning them. Throwing stones away for reasons that I can't immediately recall. Sticking leaves on cardboard trees after cutting them into "significant" shapes. Discovering that God actually spends a lot more of his time on Scottish islands than in Morrison's. Oh, for goodness' sake!

'Jack, in the course of my life I've thought about and experienced almost all the things I've just spoken about, and they led me down a road to what I can only describe as despair. It was an enormous relief to simply accept that prayer doesn't work.

'That's it. I've stopped going on now.'

Jack waited. The last of the rubbish seemed to have been cleared. He spoke very softly and with complete sincerity.

'Doc, please would you tell me all about prayer?'

'Yes. Of course. Well, I would be happy to tell you all about me and prayer.'

He paused to collect his thoughts.

'It was quite a long time ago. I was passing through London one day after visiting a friend in one of the West

End theatres who had carelessly lost himself. I had some time to waste before my train, and, like Jesus, I love wasting time, so I bought a paper – *The Times*, naturally – and parked myself with a coffee and a biro at a little table outside one of those street-side cafes. I enjoy being the still point in a turning world. Buses and taxis lurching past filled with blank-eyed people wishing they were me.

'When I got round to picking my paper up I saw that almost half the front page was taken up by a single photograph. It was a picture of a woman caught up in yet another civil war, crying over the body of her young son, shot earlier in the day by a government sniper. He was lying across her arms like a broken doll. I told you that I'm not much of a weeper, but this was another occasion when I just couldn't stop the tears from coming. I think it was something to do with her expression. She was looking straight into the camera and talking to me with her eyes. Those dark, bottomless pools of agony were filled with questions, tumbling over each other to get out.

'"What has my son done to deserve having his little life cut short by a man who probably only used him for target practice?"

'"Who on this earth is going to take the aching, crashing, sobbing pain away from my heart and my head?"

'"How am I going to move from here to somewhere else, and who will tell me when I have reached that place?"

'I broke up inside. Didn't know what to do with myself. I know I closed my eyes, and I know that I threw all my inchoate passion into the lap of God, who, for all that you have so rarely heard me speak his name, is the only receptacle I know for such torrid emotions. I may possibly have tried to frame a few specific entreaties in the course of my outpouring, but most of it was . . . it was leaning, yearning, hoping, simply wanting to be in the confluence of currents, a place where tributaries meet the main force and, however slightly, increase the power of its flow.

'Since then, Jack, there has been no question of wanting prayer to "work", although, goodness knows, I've often thought of it in that way in the past. And it's certainly nothing to do with setting some kind of spiritual machinery in motion in order to manufacture a product or prize or specific result. It's closer to paying attention to a couple of remarks made by a sane man two thousand years ago. He suggested that we should not babble on, for instance – his words, not mine. His other very sane suggestion was that you or I or anybody else should go into our room, close the door, and talk to the God who is anxious to demonstrate what being a good father really means, the God who sees how we behave when we are in our rags as well as when we wear our best clothes. It's about being with someone you love, laughing or crying or getting angry or saying nothing or falling asleep, or just identifying with that person's passionate aims and desires, whatever they might be and however little you understand them.

'So there. Prayer does not work, certainly not like a petrol pump works, or an application form or a slot machine or making a down payment. Only one thing works, and that one thing is not a thing at all. It is the one who is in control of the planning and the power. My best advice to you would be to find out what that person is doing, and to join in. If you can't work out what he is doing – join in anyway. He will be very pleased to have you.

'Do I talk to God about specific things or people? Yes I do. Every day, twice a day, for quite a while now, I have been lifting up the names and faces of quite a lot of individuals so that this same mingling, gathering process can offer as much of what is needed to each one of them as is divinely possible. Alice, your gran, was one of those until she died. You are one of them now. And last year . . . Jack, you asked me just now why I was so frightened down in the woods earlier. I'm going to tell you, but I need to ask you a question first. It's a simple one. Do you believe in the devil?'

Jack needed a break. And food. He stood up.

'I really fancy a snack. Can I get you something?'

The Shadow Doctor smiled. 'It is amazing how peckish you can get in the early hours. Why don't you put a few bits and pieces out on the table?'

Jack made toast, and set out Marmite, the remains of the whisky marmalade, and a few neglected cheese straws. Both men ate with intense enjoyment. The devil would have to wait his turn.

19

Dreaming of the Devil

Jack finished the last cheese straw, leaned across to retrieve his glass, and carefully poured out a millimetre or two of Lagavulin. Did he believe in the devil?

In fact, belief in the devil had been something like an article of faith since the day, more than two decades ago, when he had knelt at the front of an evangelistic youth meeting held in a giant blue tent in the town of Worthing in Sussex, and committed himself to following Jesus for the rest of his life. Thereafter, like a raw recruit in an unfamiliar environment, he had automatically and enthusiastically welcomed the offer of every piece of Christian equipment offered to him, concrete and abstract alike. The correct attitude to the devil was a significant item in this widely distributed kit. Satan was a lying, roaring, ever-present tempter of those believers who allowed themselves to be distracted or deflected from the path of spiritual rectitude. He existed, not in red tights and topped by a pair of horns – nobody was that deluded, for goodness' sake – but in disguise. A wolf. An angel. A shaft of deceptive light.

Until very recently Jack would have been able to answer the Shadow Doctor's question without hesitation. Of course there was a devil, and he must be resisted at all costs. All Christians were aware of that. It went without saying – or thinking, to any great extent. The thing he would not have confessed to or fully acknowledged within himself was the strange, secret pleasure that was occasionally provoked in him by the very notion of the evil one. The devil was vivid, technicolour, terrifying. He was shockingly, boldly bad, like Hitler and his Nazis. God and goodness could seem a little weak and washed out by comparison.

What was the truthful answer to Doc's question?

'I sort of think I do. We talk about him quite a bit at our church. He's in the Bible a lot, of course. Jesus mentioned him several times. We were always warned that he was out to get us, so we had to be on our guard.'

He sipped his drink, a little frightened to ask the next question.

'Why do you ask?'

The Shadow Doctor glanced in the direction of the stairs, then turned back towards Jack. There was something chilling in the emotionless monotony of his voice.

'The devil was in my dreams tonight, Jack. It was horrible. He was horrible. Vicious, appetitious, physically angular and filled with a ghastly energy. Mid-thirties, t-shirt, jeans and trainers.'

He shivered suddenly.

'I think the most unpleasant thing about this ghastly dweller in the shadows was his surprising ordinariness. There was a novel published some years ago suggesting that Sherlock Holmes and his arch-rival Moriarty were in some mysterious way light and dark sides of the same coin. I don't for one moment believe that about Jesus and the devil, but after the long, gut-wrenching experience that I've just come through I do find myself reflecting on the fact that, just as the Satan who crashed into my dreams was

repulsively ordinary, so the humanity and accessibility of
the man called Jesus has always attracted me enormously.
They both want this world with every atom of their being,
and, as they say in the television game-shows, "You have to
be in it to win it."

'I never want to go through anything like the last few
hours of my life again. I will if I have to, though. You'll
understand what that means when I tell you about the
content of my dream in a moment.

'Jack, I have to say that I feel more than a little defensive
about discussing the devil at all. Those who dismiss the
Christian faith out of hand are likely to be confirmed in
their view of us as voluntary inhabitants of Loony-land
when we trundle out the man in pantomime costume for
serious consideration. It's the same old problem, isn't it?
We who call ourselves followers of Jesus have talked about
him far too much and far too little. Evil can be such fun,
can't it?'

Jack's eyes widened.

'There has been far too much lip-licking indulgence in
the exciting prospect of the devil manifesting himself in a
variety of more or less pantomimic forms in church situations, and sometimes people relish the work of Satan without recognising him at all. A lot of so-called Christian television programmes are nothing more than spiritually
synthetic pornography. All in the name of Jesus.

'A few years ago an acquaintance of mine called Jim
went looking for help from a local Christian couple. They
told him that the chronic pain he was suffering in his jaw
was the result of devilish presence in his life. According to
them, that was why doctors had failed to come up with a

diagnosis. Dear Jim was a simple soul. He was left with a fear that the world, including his own house, and his painful jaw, was inhabited by a swarm of devils and demons.

'"I know it sounds silly, Doc," he said to me, "but I hardly dare go home. I keep looking under beds and behind the sofa to check there aren't any little grinning imps waiting to jump out at me – and my mouth still hurts like hell."'

'Were you able to help him?'

'Laughter and common sense worked pretty well in Jim's case, you'll be pleased to hear. The couple who advised him were not pleased, though. They got hold of my number and rang to complain about my attack on their so-called ministry. The conversation was shortish.'

'No, I think we say far too little about the crunching, catastrophic presence of evil in the lives of human beings every day in every part of the world. Christians rationalise and redefine like mad in order to make darkness look a little more like light, but it won't wash. Terrible, heartwrenching things happen in the immediate presence of a God who is the omnipotent source of all love. Every time we pray for people whose lives have been devastated, we are faced with the same question. Why?

'There's a verse in the first letter of John. It says that we are children of God, and that the whole world is under the control of the evil one.

'It's a paradox worthy of Chesterton, don't you think? I believe it. I believe the whole of that verse. You want me to be upfront? Here is upfront. I gratefully acknowledge that I am a child of God who will live for ever. I also see without even trying that this world is stamped all over by the one who has lost his place in heaven and is determined that as many as possible will suffer the same fate. Don't ask me to unravel the nightmare knot of logic that challenges this contention. I can't do it, Jack. What I can do is express my deeply held belief that there is one mother and father of battles being waged behind the scenes, and that we can only be truly helpful if we are realistic about the truth of those two statements.

'My dream.

'It went on for hours, waking and sleeping and waking and sleeping for what seemed an eternity. The devil was pursuing and battling for the soul of a man I have been praying for over the last few years. He's a massively popular, extremely clever man with a very good heart. He's also scathingly dismissive of the Christian faith. My job, as I saw it, was to go on and on holding his name up, without any real knowledge of where it was all going to end.

'In my dream the dismally ordinary evil one was laughing and clutching and claiming and drooling over what he saw as the inevitability of victory. Every time I woke I prayed clumsily and frantically for this person whom God seems to want so much. Each time I slept again I went back to a world where some kind of gigantic question was being asked, and perhaps beginning to be answered.

'What was the outcome of all that? I have no idea. I would go through it again if necessary, but my nervous plea to God is one uttered by Jesus himself. If possible, please take it away. Tell me I don't have to go through the fire. Nevertheless, if you say I must – I will.'

He remained motionless for a few seconds, then shifted in his chair.

'I really must go to bed.'

20

The Hostage

'Can I ask you one more thing?'

'You'd make a good Columbo, Jack. Yes, of course you can.'

'Why did you relegate Vanessa to the spare bedroom?'

Doc's tired face creased and fell into an expression of such sadness that Jack immediately wished he had never asked the question. It had been intended as a flippancy, a way to dispel some of the darkness that had filled the kitchen as the other man spoke of the devil in such immanent, personal terms.

The Shadow Doctor sat back down on his chair, his gaze fixed on some invisible spot on the wall above the range. His reply came almost in a whisper.

'She and I had a falling out. One of us had to go.'

Jack studied the stone-flagged floor. Another dose of misery. If this strange relationship really was going to continue, he would need to find some way to strengthen his core, build some genuine muscles of survival. When he raised his head, Doc was very gently waving the whisky bottle.

'Let's have that other very small one before we go up the wooden hill, Jack. If I don't get to sleep soon I shall fall off this chair. I'm sure you feel the same. Push your glass over here. Yes? Good, there we are. Welcome to the flow, by the way. I'm going to give you a hostage now, and then I'm going to ask you one last question before we go to bed. OK?'

'OK. A hostage?'

Reflected light in the Shadow Doctor's eyes seemed to swim a little as he struggled to embark on whatever it was he had decided to say. Unshed tears? Just listen, Jack said firmly to himself. Don't make it about you. Just listen.

'One night I decided to drive that wonderful photograph of Vanessa Redgrave down through the forest to the reservoir, weight it somehow and make sure I never saw it again. In the end I couldn't do it. I got as far as the landing and stood outside my bedroom door like a child stranded in the middle of the night, balancing that great big picture against my body with one hand and . . . and crying in the dark like a baby. I keep saying I don't cry. I do. I did then.

'The thing is, young Vanessa is the spitting – I'd prefer to say the kissing – image of the person I loved most in the world. My wife. My best friend. She gave it to me. Every single morning after the brain tumour killed her and I was left on my own, that picture – that face, with its teasing, challenging smile – was up there on my bedroom wall waiting to greet me. It was too much and far, far too little. In the end I couldn't bear the thought of drowning poor sweet Vanessa, so I put her in your room.'

'My room?'

'Well, it wasn't your room then, of course, but, in a way, that brings me to my question. It's not a new one, but I think I need an answer now. Do you want to move in full time and work with me, Jack? I'm afraid it would be very unpredictable and odd, as well as being fairly tedious on occasions, but as I said to you on the evening when you first visited, you and I have been living on very lonely little islands. Perhaps we would be able to move towards each other until we can meet at a place where both of us are more or less authentic and safe. Not safe in any way that the rest of the world is likely to understand, and certainly not authentic in the sense that we know exactly what to say or do. God forbid. He certainly will.

'So that's it. I need a travelling companion, and, though I find it ridiculously hard to admit, a friend. There, I've said it. I need a friend, Jack, but only if he needs my company and can put up with me as well. What do you think? A challenge for people as different as you and me, and, as we've discovered, we are really going to get on each other's nerves at times, but both of us are looking for solid ground, and the search should be interesting, to say the least. Lots of adventures, I can promise you that. I do need you, Jack, and I suspect that you might benefit from being with me.' He smiled. 'Sorry, I'm in danger of repeating myself fifty-five times.'

Jack pushed his empty glass away across the table, unconsciously dismissing any element of frivolity from the conversation.

'Thank you for the hostage.'

Doc inclined his head graciously.

'She must have been very beautiful.'

'Inside and out.'

'You and she had a cat and a dog.'

'We did.'

'The bantams were hers.'

'They were.'

'Did you ask God to make her better?'

'My emails must have gone astray.'

'I'm so sorry.'

'I'll tell you one good thing, Jack.'

'Yes?'

'She would have loved my new bright orange scarf.'

Ask him to speak her name.

Jack had become conscious of a gentle vibrancy inhabiting the air of the room. It reminded him of another occasion. At first the detail escaped him, then he remembered. It was the moment when Doc had posed his crossword clue to Daniel Tressingham – or Christopher Marsh, as he turned out to be. The clue had been something about compassion. The solution had been 'mercy'. He cleared his throat.

'What was her name – your wife, I mean?'

The Shadow Doctor's head jerked to one side, as if his face had been lightly slapped. He clenched his fist tightly before slowly releasing it and allowing his hand to lie flat on the table, as if in submission.

'Her name was . . . Miriam. My wife's name was Miriam, Jack. I haven't spoken her name aloud for . . . oh, it must be fifteen years.'

'I wish . . .'

'Oh, so do I. Tell me, Jack, have you ever been in love?'

Jack clenched everything. Blurred images rushed through his head. 'Not . . . no, not really. I don't think so.'

'A risky business in all sorts of ways. I mean, if you're not in possession of something incredibly valuable there's not much danger of losing it. What do you say? Should I pray that you will or that you will not be faced with that wonderful, terrible risk?'

'It makes no difference,' said Jack. 'You seem to have forgotten that prayer doesn't work.'

The Shadow Doctor chuckled as he reached for his coat and rose to his feet.

'True enough. Hoist on my own whatsit. Do you have an answer to my other question, Jack? Just think what you'd miss. First meeting of the Marsh-Wiggle Club. Joining me when I drop in on Victor. And, in the not-too-distant future, I have to pay a visit to a very well-known Christian leader. I'm afraid I'm likely to seriously spoil his day. Oh, and I don't know if your gran mentioned it in the letter she left you, but something very significant happened to her shortly before her death. I think it could make you very happy. Stay, and I might tell you what it was. Perhaps that's unfair. Now you have no choice. Tell me you'll come, Jack. I need you.'

'Is George in agreement?'

His question seemed to take the older man aback.

'Ah, now that's a good question. Yes, I believe he is.'

'If I stay, will you tell me who George is, what the calls mean, where Martha fits into everything, how it all began – that stuff?'

A serious moment. Doc transferred his coat from one arm to the other yet again and expelled a breath through expanded cheeks.

'Too complicated for now. And a little too strange. It takes some believing. Eventually, yes. I shall have to.'

'I would like to stay – I mean, I think I will stay. I mean, I will stay.'

'I'm so glad. Thank you, Jack. Put your nets on eBay in the morning. I'm going up now. Say hello to Vanessa for me when you see her. Goodnight.'

'Goodnight, Doc.'

Jack sat in the warm kitchen for another half hour, waiting for the turmoil in his breast to subside. He felt as if he had taken an over-bold step, something like signing up for service on an alien spacecraft. Where would the journey take him? Who was in charge? How would it all end? Why hadn't he asked anything about money? What would he live on? Abandoning those unanswerable questions at last, he carefully locked the door to keep the devil out and the Shadow Doctor happy, turned off the oven and the lights, kicked his shoes off at the bottom of the stairs and hoisted himself up the steep steps towards bed. One of his last thoughts before drifting into unconsciousness was another question. What had the Shadow Doctor meant about putting his nets on eBay? He must remember to ask him in the morning. As a very comfortable sleep carried him gently away, he had the strangest sense that he could hear his gran laughing in the far distance. It was nice. It made him smile.

'Oh! Nets. Of course . . .'

On the other side of the landing, the Shadow Doctor had turned his covers down. Before getting into what he still thought of as his side of the bed, he walked self-consciously around to the far side and picked up a novel from the little table near the window. Carefully removing the bookmark, and averting his eyes in order not to accidentally register the page number, he kissed the front of the dusty volume very gently as he made his way back across the room and returned it to a gap in the bookcase beside his bedroom door. Climbing into bed at last, he took a last look around the room, then reached wearily above his head and turned out the light.

Acknowledgements

I am very grateful to Ian Metcalfe for his great patience and fine editing skills, and to my wife Bridget for her even greater patience as this book was finally and painfully brought to a conclusion.

Credits

Do you wish this wasn't the end?
Are you hungry for more great teaching, inspiring
testimonies, ideas to challenge your faith?

Join us at www.hodderfaith.com, follow us on Twitter
or find us on Facebook to make sure you get the latest from
your favourite authors.

Including interviews, videos, articles, competitions
and opportunities to tell us just what you thought about
our latest releases.

www.hodderfaith.com

HodderFaith

@HodderFaith

HodderFaithVideo

HODDER
WHERE FAITH IS INSPIRED